Anonymity
in Western Literature

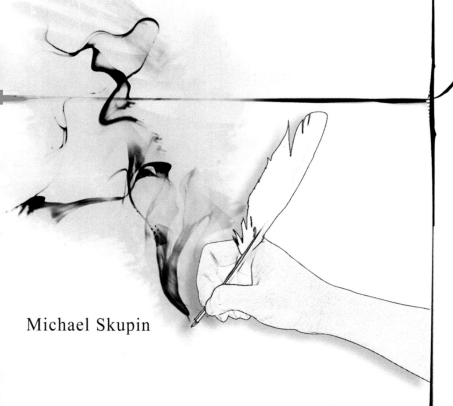

Michael Skupin

Introduction

What's in a name?

Many, many years ago, when I first began reading what is now called the canon, those literary works that one must know in order to be considered literate, I remember being puzzled from time to time by extra-literary clutter. Byron was very handsome, I was told; Dante Gabriel Rosetti was also a talented painter. I did not understand what Byron's looks had to do with the excellence of his writing, nor did I understand how Rosetti's brush was supposed to brush over the fact that I found his poetry boring. The message was clear, though: the author's name is a trademark, a brand. Yet a brand implies consistency, and my subsequent reading showed me time and again that literature is not so predictable. To cite only one example, most of the work of Philip Freneau, "the poet of the American Revolution," is pseudoclassical bombast, and justly forgotten, but in midst of the slag is his abolitionist poem "Sir Toby," a gem. I found that the opposite was also true: there are times when good Homer does indeed nod. When my reading progressed to comparing authors' published writings with their private letters, I was shocked to discover what is called the persona, that is, the way a writer wants to be thought of as opposed to the way he is. Put more crudely, the persona is the lie that the writer tells his readers. E.A. Robinson talked about being objective, but, as I point out in my book *Merlin, Merlin, Merlin*, he never wrote an objective line in his life; his younger contemporary Frost presented himself as countrified old Uncle Robert, but his correspondence revealed a personality that was belligerent, even corrosive. Yet Frost's lyrics, like "The Road Not Taken," will be read for as long as the English language is spoken, and Robinson's epics, like *Tristram,* are literary landmarks that will endure, after they are rediscovered by a new generation, that is, since they are too taxing for the critics and editors of today, who think on the scale of the poesy of a ring; on the scale of the poesy of a fortune cookie.

In the case of Freneau, Robinson and Frost, the author's signature becomes misleading, a distortion of the work. This leads to other questions of attribution: first, is the attribution factually correct? Did the author of *As You Like It* really write *Titus Andronicus*? If it were discovered that *As You Like It* was in fact written by one of Shakespeare's contemporaries, say, George Peele, would that make *As You Like It* a lesser play? Taken a step further, without Shakespearean authorship, would *Titus Andronicus* be performed at all?

Second, what if there is no attribution? That is the case with the Anglo-Saxon poems discussed in this study. *Phoenix, Christ and Satan* and *Beowulf* are anonymous, but although unsigned, each reveals the personality of its author between the lines.

What if there is an attribution, but one that is only a name, with perhaps a few scraps of historical fact? This is the case with the second work, *Pelagius.* We are given an author's name, Hrotsvit of Gandersheim (or Hrotswith, or Roswitha, among other variants), but nothing else. Much scholarly squinting at her corpus suggests a hazy sort of context (the tenth-century court of the German emperor Otto I), but nothing definite about the author. All we can know of her is what we can intuit from her work, whether a portrayal of Moorish Cordoba (the subject of *Pelagius*), or any of the other themes she treats, and which, I would argue, reveal a consistent personality. Although Hrotsvit of Gandersheim has long been known for her Latin dramas, recent scholarship has drawn attention to her saints' lives and epics. Of particular interest is *Pelagius*, which is one of the earliest North European accounts of Islam, being set in Moslem Spain. Aside from its literary excellence, the poem is a window on the times: Hrotsvit states that her story is a versification of an eyewitness account of that saint's martyrdom, and the diplomatic contacts between the court of Otto I and the caliph of Cordoba, Abd ar-Rahman III, evidently provided her with background information. Hrotsvit's *Pelagius*, then, preserves a contemporary view of Moorish society from the perspective of a very sophisticated writer; equally instructive are Hrotsvit's errors, omissions and editorializing, which makes *Pelagius* a sermon to the Ottonian court. Yet all we can know of the author is what we can intuit from her work, so *Pelagius* is, to all intents and purposes, as anonymous as *Phoenix*.

The *Vita Merlini* ("Merlin's Life") is another example of an authorial attribution being a distortion. As long as this medieval Latin epic was attributed to Geoffrey of Monmouth, no proper understanding of the poem was possible, because the learnèd were fixated on resolving the inconsistencies between the *Vita Merlini* and Geoffrey's more famous *Historia Regum Britanniae* ("History of the Kings of Britain"). Restoring the poem to anonymity is the first step to reading the poem without preconceptions.

William Shakespeare has a place in this study because of the "crit" inspired by *Titus Andronicus*.   A play this bad could not possibly be by Shakespeare, went the reasoning, so there must be an unknown hand involved.   This is anonymity as a fig leaf.

Grimm's Fairy Tales are almost as famous as the plays of the Bard, but the matter of anonymity involves them, too.   The Brothers Grimm did not claim to be authors, but collectors of folklore.   All but two of their sources are unnamed, and there is uncertainty about the extent and nature of the contributions of these two.   Who, then, is the author?   Is there, in fact, an author in the commonly-accepted meaning of the word?   How much of the Grimms is in *Grimm's Fairy Tales*?

This book began as a collection of papers I have presented at conferences in Taiwan, while teaching at Chinese Culture University.   CCU is a school unusually conducive to writing, both for its stimulating intellectual life and for the beauty – and oxygen – of its location on a high ridge overlooking Taipei on one side and a magnificent national park on the other.   Taiwan is conducive to writing, because my counterparts at other universities are accomplished scholars, the sort of audience for whom one wants to give his best.   In addition to the conference papers, I have interpolated shorter pieces that are echoes, as it were, of the longer pieces' themes.

A wag might make fun of an author who writes a book on anonymity and then signs his name to it.   That will not seem such a contradiction after reading this book, so I do, in fact, sign it, hoping that the reader will enjoy reading it as much as I have enjoyed writing it.

Michael Skupin
Taipei, Taiwan, ROC
December 3, 2008

Table of Contents

Reclaimed Anonymity:

The *Vita Merlini* Poet and Isidore of Seville

I concede at the outset that the scholarly consensus accepts without question that Geoffrey of Monmouth, the author of the famous prose *Historia Regum Britanniae* ("The History of the Kings of England," to be abbreviated *HRB*) is also the author of the lesser-known 1,529 line epic *Vita Merlini* ("Merlin's Life," to be abbreviated as *VM*). I dissent from the consensus, however, maintaining, first, that the author of *VM* is unknown, and second, that even as a "default" candidate, Geoffrey of Monmouth is not first in line. In this case, authorship is not merely a superficial matter of labeling; Geoffrey comes with so much "baggage" (because of the fame of *HRB* and its message) that the reader of *VM* is distracted by intrusive questions like "Why does Geoffrey say this in *VM*, when in *HRB* he said that?" It is important to explicitly remove Geoffrey as author in order to see the *VM* without preconceptions.

There are only two arguments for Galfridian authorship that are not *a priori,* one based on the last five lines of the poem, the other on the work's dedication. John Parry, distinguished translator and editor of medievalia in the early part of the last century (and, I concede, an advocate of Geoffrey as a default candidate), expresses the first contention thus:

The one definite piece of evidence in regard to the authorship of the poem is contained in the last five lines...This seems quite evidently intended as an attribution of the poem to Geoffrey of Monmouth, and although found in only one manuscript (*Cotton Vespasian E 14,* the earliest and only complete one), it is there in the same handwriting as the rest, and seems to have formed part of the original text.[1]

Let us examine these five lines.

Duximus ad metam carmen vos ergo britanni 1525.

We have led this song to its end.

You, therefore, Britons,

Laurea serta date Gaufrido de Monumeta
Est etenim vester nam quondam prelia vestra
Vestrorum que ducum cecinit scripsit que libellum

Give a laurel wreath to Geoffrey of Monmouth, For he is yours, and formerly your wars And your leaders has he sung, and wrote a little book

Quem nunc gesta vocant britonum celebrata per orbem.

Which now they call The Deeds of the Britons, renowned throughout the world.

We note, first of all, that these lines contradict Parry's claim that they formed part of the original text: line 1525 has "we" as the subject and the next line has Geoffrey of Monmouth as the

---

[1] Parry 9.

indirect object. "We" must be either the editorial "we" or it is "we" in the sense of "you (the reader) and I (the author)." Let us stick to knowns: in the dedication to the *VM,* the author refers to himself in the first person singular, not with the editorial "we," so, unless we wish play it deuces wild, rigor requires that we take the editorial "we" off the table. This leaves only "we" in the sense of "you (the reader) and I (the author)," which is the subject of the sentence, as distinct from the indirect object, which is "Geoffrey;" and therefore "Geoffrey" is neither "you (the reader)" nor is he "I (the author)." The last five lines are not an attribution of authorship at all, but an encomium.

Parry expresses his other argument thus:

> Even without these concluding lines there would have been a presumption that Geoffrey was the author because of the reference in the dedication to an earlier work, dedicated by the author of this one to Robert's predecessor as Bishop of Lincoln, that had not met with the reception that was expected... Bishop Alexander to whom, as is well known, Geoffrey dedicated his *Prophecies of Merlin,* and who appears to have done nothing for him.[2]

In point of fact, however, Alexander is not mentioned by name; the text simply refers to *alter,* "the other," as the relevant lines in the dedication make plain.

---

[2] Parry 9-10.

Ergo meis ceptis faueas	Therefore, may you sponsor
vatemque tueri	what I have begun and protect
	the poet
Auspicio meliore velis quam	With better offices, if you
fecerit alter	please, than the other would
	have done,
Cui modo succedis merito	He whom you are succeeding
promotus honori.	because of merit, promoted to
	the honor.

It is also to be noted that there is no mention of a prior dedication, either.

This, however, is incidental to the real flaw in Parry's argument, his assumption that the uniqueness of the dedicatee proves the uniqueness of the dedicator. Granting that the *VM* is dedicated to Robert, Bishop of Lincoln, successor to Alexander of that title, and granting that the same Alexander was the one in Geoffrey's *HRB,* and even granting that the said Robert and Alexander are the only possible dedicatees, in what sense does this point to Geoffrey of Monmouth and only Geoffrey of Monmouth as the dedicator?

As a thought experiment, I propose to show that Henry of Huntingdon is a more likely candidate than Geoffrey of Monmouth. I am not advancing this archdeacon's candidacy for authorship of the *VM;* I believe that the *VM*'s authorship is unknown. I am simply illustrating how flimsy the Galfridian claim is, even against a non-candidate. On Henry's behalf I need offer nothing more than Diana Greenway's excellent edition of his *Historia Anglorum* ("History of the English People," to be abbreviated *HA*). I will begin with two of

Parry's own criteria, the matter of Robert and Alexander, then go on to parameters where Henry is strong and where Geoffrey is a virtual no-show, and rest my case with the matter of the encomium.

Was Robert de Chesney, the dedicatee of the *VM,* "once an Oxford colleague of Geoffrey?"[3]   Well and good; but Henry's relationship with Robert, a fellow churchman, is known to have lasted for many years: Henry refers to him four times in *HA*, including a description of his investiture as Bishop of Lincoln, and thus as Henry's superior, that is similar to the dedication of the *VM.*   Note the phrases I have underlined.

> *A cunctis igitur honore tanto dignus habitus <u>rege et clero et populo cum summo gaudio annuente</u>... et in Epiphania Domini apud Lincoliam cum summo tripudio magnus expectatione, <u>maior adventu a clero et populo cum devotione suscepto est.</u>   Prosperet ei Deus tempora prava, et <u>iuuentutem eius foveat rore sapientie</u>...*
> *("He was universally considered worthy of so great an honor, and <u>with the very joyful approval of king, clergy and people</u>...and with great jubilation he was eagerly awaited and <u>still more eagerly welcomed, being devotedly received by clergy and people</u> at Lincoln at the Lord's Epiphany [6 January 1149].   May God favour him in evil times, and <u>nourish his young days with the dew of wisdom</u>...")* [4]

---

[3]   Clark 136.
[4]   HA 752-5.

Compare this with the *VM:*

scimus enim <u>quis te perfudit</u>	For we know <u>what has anointed</u>
<u>nectare sacro</u>	<u>you with its holy nectar:</u>
Philosophia suo fecitque per	Philosophy, and it has made
omnia doctum... 5.	you learnèd throughout all
	[fields],...

Mutatis mutandis, philosophy for wisdom and nectar for dew, the passages are reminiscent of each other. The reference to clergy and people is a clearer echo.

Sic etenim mores sic vita	Yea, indeed [your] behavior, yea,
probata genusque 10.	your upright life and family
Utilitasque loci <u>clerus</u>	And efficiency of your office, <u>the</u>
<u>populusque petebant.</u>	<u>clergy and laity [all] sought [it].</u>

To be fair, there is a passage in the opening (219) of the "vulgate" *Historia Regum Britanniae* (*HRB*) that is similar to the *VM*'s dedication. First, the *VM.*

<u>tu corrige carmen</u> 2.	<u>Correct the song,</u> you,
Gloria pontificum calamos	Robert, glory of the priesthood,
moderando roberte	by guiding my pen,
scimus enim quis te <u>perfudit</u>	For we know what has <u>anointed</u>
<u>nectare sacro</u>	<u>you with its holy nectar:</u>
<u>Philosophia</u> suo fecitque	<u>Philosophy,</u> and it has made
per omnia doctum 5.	you learnèd throughout all
	[fields],

HRB has *Opusculo igitur meo Roberte dux claudiocestrie faveas. ut sic te doctore te monitore <u>corrigatur</u>... quem <u>philosophia</u> liberalibus artibus <u>erudivit</u>...* ("O Robert, duke of Gloucester, may you be well disposed toward my little work...so that, thus, with you the teacher, you the adviser, <u>it will be corrected</u>...[you] whom <u>philosophy has nurtured</u> in the liberal arts..."). As a cautionary note, a dedication is not much to build on: in the Bern version of *HRB* the foregoing dedication note is addressed not to Robert of Gloucester, but to King Stephen (with a secondary dedication to Robert, *altera regni nostra columna* ["the other pillar of our kingdom"]); another group of *HRB* manuscripts has a double dedication to Robert and to Waleran of Meulan.[5]

On the other hand, there the matter, minor, but worth noting, of *gloria pontificum* in line 3 above; Henry used the phrase *pontificum Robertus honor* ("Robert, honor of the priesthood") in the epitaph he wrote at Robert's death. Still, I will concede that the dedication to Robert would favor Geoffrey just as much as Henry, although, it should be remembered that Henry is a non-candidate.

As for Alexander, it is true that Geoffrey dedicated the section of *HRB* concerned with the prophecies of Merlin to him, but it is also true that Alexander is the dedicatee of the whole of Henry's *HA,* that he is mentioned more than a dozen times in *HA,* by my count, and, more to the point, that he is addressed by Henry in dactylic hexameter, with phrases that seem to echo the *VM.*

O decus, <u>o morum directio</u>, quo veniente...
Leue iugum, doctrina placens, <u>correctio dulcis</u>,...

---

[5] Wright 1:xiii.

Lincolie gens magna prius, nunc maxima semper... (HA 474)

("O ornament, <u>o uprightness of behavior</u>, at whose coming...light yoke, pleasing teaching, <u>sweet correction</u>...O <u>people of Lincoln</u>, previously great, <u>now forever greatest</u>...")

In addition to the already-noted correction motiv, there are two other echoes of the above in *VM*, mutatis mutandis:

Sic etenim <u>mores</u> sic <u>vita</u> *<u>probata</u> genusque*	10.	Yea, indeed [your] <u>behavior</u>, yea, your <u>upright life</u> and family
Unde modo felix <u>lincolnia</u> *fertur ad astra.*	12.	Hence, <u>happy Lincoln is carried to the stars.</u>

This is especially damning to Geoffrey's candidacy because nowhere in *HRB* does Geoffrey show the slightest talent for verse, or even the slightest interest in poetry at all.   The only way to make him a poet is by circular reasoning, that Geoffrey had the poetic talent to write the *VM* because the *VM* is commonly attributed to him, which, given the poetic excellence of the *VM*, means that those moderns who make him its author by default are also making him an excellent poet by default.   Henry of Huntingdon's poetic skill is a matter of record.

Henry is also known to have composed versifications of scientific subjects,[6] and it is known that the Lincoln chapter

---

[6] *HA* cxiv.

library contained Isidore of Seville's *Etymologies*; [7] long passages in the *VM* are skillful and very close versifications of Isidore's scientific essays. On Geoffrey's side: nothing.

Henry is known to have been part of the "Ovidian subculture" of his day, not only by his contacts with contemporary Ovidians,[8] but by his own poetry written in imitation of Ovid.[9] The *VM* (lines 191-197) specifically alludes to Ovid's *Heroides,* a minor work much less well-known than the *Metamorphoses.* On Geoffrey's side: nothing.

Finally, there is the matter of the *VM* encomium, the five-line tag at the end of the poem that praises Geoffrey of Monmouth. *HA* also contains an encomium that praises Geoffrey, this after an overview of British prehistory:

> Hec sunt que tibi brevibus promisi. Quorum si prolixitatem desideras, librum grandem Galfredi Arturi, quem apud Beccum inveni, queras. Vbi predicta diligenter et prolixe tractata videbis.
>
> ("These are the matters I promised you in brief. If you would like them at length, you should ask for Geoffrey Arthur's great book, which I discovered at Le Bec. There you will find a careful and comprehensive treatment of the above.")[10]

On Geoffrey's side: nothing, unless his defensiveness *vis-à-vis* his peers be taken as a compliment. *Reges vero saxonum*

---

[7] *HA* xxxii.
[8] *HA* xxxv.
[9] *HA* 818ff.
[10] *HA* 582-3.

Willelmo malmesberiensi & henrico huntendonensi quos de regibus britonum tacere iubeo ("[the subject of] the kings of the Saxons I leave to William of Malmesbury and Henry of Huntingdon, both of whom I command to be silent on the subject of the kings of the Britons") (*HRB* 536), since neither of them had seen the alleged *vetustissimus liber* ("very old book") that Geoffrey claimed as his source.

I repeat that I am not trying to show that Henry of Huntingdon wrote the *VM.* I have tried to show that default candidate Geoffrey compares unfavorably with Henry, who is not even a candidate. It is time to retire the *VM's* Galfridian attribution and simply state that its authorship is unknown, which will allow us to concentrate on the poem without preconceptions.

The *VM* poet, as I will henceforth call him, may not have a name, but he does have a personality, as can be judged by comparing his finished "product" with the literary raw material he used. It has long been recognized that *VM* contains three passages that derive directly from Isidore of Seville's *Etymologies.* It will be fruitful to examine these passages in detail, and discuss the technical virtuosity shown in transforming good Latin prose into fine Latin poetry.

The reader unfamiliar with this fine medieval epic is referred to two sources, John J. Parry's annotated *en face* translation, and to my dissertation, which has a close parallel translation and a discussion of the work as a source of twentieth century poet Laurence Binyon's drama *The Madness of Merlin.*

I trust that the reader familiar with Latin poetry will indulge a few prefatory remarks about dactylic hexameter, the meter of the *Vita Merlini.* If this is redundant, so be it; I had rather include readers than exclude them.

Dactylic hexameter, the rhythm *par excellence* of epic poetry, consists of six-beat lines of dactyls (a long syllable followed by two short ones) and spondees (two long syllables). Ovid (known to the *VM* poet) used it for light-hearted themes, but more commonly it is used as did Virgil (also known to the *VM* poet), for themes of weight and dignity. The poet controls the tempo by balancing the ictus (the tick-tock regular rhythm) and the accent (the natural stress of the words). When ictus and accent match, the motion of the verse is fast and smooth; when they clash, the movement is slow, with syncopated "kicks." The author's challenge is to fit the poetic means with the poetic message.

As stated above, on three occasions the *VM* poet took on another challenge, that of versifying the prose of encyclopedist Isidore of Seville. He did so successfully, and his achievement is remarkable both for the ingenuity of the circumlocutions he employed and for the fidelity to Isidore's text that will be demonstrated. *VM* 875-909 derive from Isidore's XIV.vi, *De insulis* ("concerning islands"), *VM* 1179-1242 from Isidore's XIII.xiii, *De diversitate aquarum*, ("concerning the diversity of bodies of water"), and *VM* 1301-1386 from Isidore's XII.vii, *De avibus* ("concerning birds"), which amount to just over 10% of the *VM* in all. This will be our starting point.

When the VM poet came to Isidore's parrot, he found a physical description, a mention of its talent for mimicry, and a reference in the poet Martial. He chose the second.

> *Vnde et articulata verba exprimit, ita ut si eam non videris,*
> *hominem loqui putes. Ex natura autem salutat dicens:*
> *"have" vel χαῖρε.*

("And thence [from the size of its tongue] it expresses spoken words; thus, if you did not see it, you would think a man was speaking. From its nature, however, it greets [you], saying "hail" or "hello" [in Greek]")

This is versified by elegant circumlocutions: *articulata verba* becomes *humanam vocem* ("human speech"), *exprimit* becomes *proprio modulamine* ("by its own call"), *ut si eam non videris* becomes *dum non spectatur* ("while not being seen"), and *putes* becomes *putatur* ("it is thought"). The poet includes the greetings without much ado.

Psitacus humanam proprio modulamine vocem	1362	The parrot's voice is sometimes mistaken for a human's
Dum non spectatur prorsus proferre putatur		While not being directly observed.
Intermiscet ave verbis et chere iocosis		It mixes "hello" and "bonjour" with joking words.

The poet is equally selective in his treatment of Isidore's pelican, omitting the account of the bird's habitat and name. He focuses instead on the most arresting details.

Fertur, si verum sit, eam occidere natos suos, eosque per triduum lugere, deinde se ipsam vulnerare et aspersione sui sanguinis vivificare filios.

> ("It is said, if it be true, that it kills its young, and
> mourns them for a three-day period; afterward it
> wounds itself, and by sprinkling its blood revives
> its children.")

Pelicanus is inflated to *pelicanus avis* ("the pelican-bird"), *natos suos* becomes *pullos* ("chicks"), *occidere* becomes *necare* ("slay"), *triduum* becomes *tribus diebus* ("for three days"), *se vulnere* becomes *laniat sua corpora* ("tears its bodies" [plural for singular, as frequently in Virgil]) and *scindens venas* ("cutting veins"), and *aspersione sui sanguinis* is theatrically rendered by *rorando* ("dripping") and *educit sanguinis undas* ("leads forth waves of blood.")

Est pelicanus avis pullos	1365.	The pelican is a bird
consueta necare		accustomed to kill its
		young,
Et confusa tribus lugere		And mourn in grief for
dolore diebus		three days.
Denique supposito laniat		Thereafter it tears its own
sua corpora rostro		body with its beak,
Et scindens venas educit		And, cutting the veins, lets
sanguinis undas		out waves of blood,
Et vite reduces reddit		And the birds are quickly
rorando volucres		returned to life by the
		dripping.

Isidore is at pains to distinguish between *pica* ("magpie") and *picus* ("woodpecker"), but the *VM* poet immediately concentrates on the latter.

Picus a Pico Saturni filio nomen sumpsit, eo quod eam in auspiciis utebatur.   Nam ferunt hanc avem quiddam habere divinum, illo indicio quod in quacumque arbore nidificaverit, clavum, vel quidquid alium fixum, diu haerere non potest quin statim excidat ubi ea insederit.

> ("The woodpecker [picus] took over the name of Picus the son of Saturn, by which that [bird? Isisdore's antecedent is not clear] is used in divination.   For, they say, this bird has something of the divine, as shown by the fact that in whatever tree it makes its nest, a nail, or anything else driven in, cannot stay stuck in long, for immediately it pops out where the bird settles.")

The *VM* poet retouches the above by replacing the vague *alium* with the specific *cuneos* ("wedges"), by concretizing *excidat* with *quos non divelleret ullus* ("which no one else could tear out"), and adding a description of the woods ringing with the bird's hammering.

Quando nidificat devellit		When the woodpecker nests,
ab arbore picus		it tears from the tree
Clavos et cuneos quos	1385.	Nails and wedges which no
non divelleret ullus		other can tear out;
Cuius ab impulsu vicinia		The area around resounds
tota resultant		with his blows.

Isidore also describes birds whose nomenclature is uncertain, and which have supernatural characteristics.   His account of the "hercynia" makes a passing mention of the bird's origin, but goes immediately to the miraculous.

> *Hercyniae aves dictae ab Hercynio saltu Germaniae, ubi nascuntur, quarum pinnae adeo per obscurum emicant ut quamvis nox obtenta densis tenebris sit, ad praesidium itineris dirigendi praeiactae interluceant, cursusque viae pateat indicio plumarum fulgentium.*

("Hercynia-birds are so called from the Hercynian wood in Germany, where they are born; whose feathers thus shine through the dark so that however dark and thick with shadows the night may be, they throw forth beams as a safeguard of the path that must be followed, and the course of the way is clearly seen by the flashings of the feathers.")

The *VM* poet opts for singular for plural here, *pennam* ("feather") for *pinnae*, omits the bird's habitat as before, downplays Isidore's description of the night and chooses a stronger simile for brightness, *ignea lampas* ("fiery torch"), for *praesidium itineris* has *ministrat iter* ("furnishes a way"), and pads the line with an extra verb and a personification, *si preportetur eunti* ("if carried before the traveler").

Fert quoque mirandam splendens hircinea pennam Nocte sub obscura que fulget ut ignea lampas Atque ministrat iter si preportetur eunti	1381	The radiant Hercynia carries an amazing feather, Which shines in the dark night like a fiery torch And shows the way if carried before the traveler.

Another fabulous bird is the halcyon.   Isidore makes no distinction between its habitat, the site of its wonders, and his forced etymology of the bird's name (*alcyon*=<u>al</u>[e]<u>s o</u>[cea]<u>n</u>[ea], "ocean-wing").

> *Alcyon pelagi volucris dicta, quasi ales oceanea, eo quod hieme in stagnis oceani nidos facit pullosque educit ; qua excubante fertur extento aequore pelagus silentibus ventis continua septem dierum tranquillitate mitescere, et eius fetibus educandis obsequium ipsa rerum natura praebere.*
>
> ("The halcyon is said to be a sea bird, wings of the sea, as it were, which in winter makes its nest in ocean pools and raises its chicks; while brooding, it is said, all across the deep the winds are silent, and the ocean is calm for seven days running, and it offers itself to the raising of its hatchlings in accordance with its own nature.")

The *VM* poet changes *stagnis oceani* to *stagna marina frequentat* ("frequents maritime pools"), *silentibus ventis* to *venti cessant* ("winds cease"), *hieme* to *hiemale tempore* ("in wintertime"), and shortens *qua excubante* to *dum cubat* ("while it nests").

Alcion avis est que stagna marina frequentat	The halcyon is a bird that frequents maritime pools
Edificat que suos hiemale tempore nidos	And builds its nests in winter.
Dum cubat equora sunt septem tranquilla diebus	While it nests, the seas are calm for seven days

Et venti cessant tempestates	1360.	And the winds cease, and
que remisse		storms hold back, to
		produce
Inpendunt placidam volucri		A placid calm for the
famulando quietem		nesting bird.

Isidore tells us nothing about the appearance, habitat or call of the "cinnamolgus." He provides a description of its nesting habits, however, as a continuation of his account of the phoenix, and its nest of spices.

> *Cinnamolgus et ipsa Arabiae avis, proinde ita vocata quod in excelsis nemoribus texit nidos ex fruticibus cinnami: et quoniam non possunt ibi homines conscendere propter ramorum altitudinem et fragilitatem, eosdem nidos plumbatis appetunt iaculis, ac sic cinnama illa deponunt, et pretiis amplioribus vendunt; [eo] quod cinnamum magis quam alia mercatores vendunt.*
>
> ("The cinnamolgus and that very bird of Arabia, in the same way is thus called because in the highest groves builds nests of cinnamon twigs: and because men cannot climb there on account of the height and fragility of the branches, they attack those same nests with lead-weighted darts, and thus bring down the cinnamon sticks, and sell them at a very high price, because merchants sell cinnamon more than other merchandise.")

The VM poet particularizes the image, *procero robore* ("in a high oak") for *in excelsis nemoribus.* He also makes a mistake with his darts, misreading *plumbatis* ("weighted with lead") as *plumatis* ("plumed"), which leads to the paraphrase *pennatis telis* ("with feathered weapons"). Subjectively speaking, I find this sort of error harmless, even endearing; objectively speaking, it is a mark of authenticity, since it is a slip that would never occur to a modern forger.

Nidificare volens fert		The cinnamolgus, wishing
cinnomon cinomolgus		to nest, brings cinnamon
Edificat que suum procero		And builds its nest in a
robore nidum		high oak.
Illinc pennatis homines	1355.	From there men with
abducere telis		feathered weapons attempt
Moverunt cumulum soliti		To take away the heap,
transmittere venum		accustomed to take it
		away for sale.

On the subject of bodies of water, Isidore mentions thirty noteworthy sites:

1. The Albulan waters, near Rome.
2. The Fountain of Cicero, in Italy.
3. A lake in Ethiopia.
4. Zama, a spring in Africa.
5. Lake Clitorius, in Italy.
6. A spring in Chios.
7. Two springs in Boeothia.
8. A spring named Cyzicus.
9. A lake in Boeothia.
10. Waters in Campagna.
11. A spring in Ethiopia.
12. Leinus, a spring in Arcadia.

13. Two springs in Sicily.
14. Two rivers in Thessaly.
15. Clitumnus, a lake in Umbria.
16. The Reatine swamp.
17. The "Asphalt Lake" in Judaea.
18. Side, a pond in India.
19. Apuscidamus, a lake in Africa.
20. The spring of Marsidas, in Phrygia.
21. The water called Styx, in Achaia.
22. The Gelonian pond, in Sicily.
23. A spring in Africa around the temple of Ammon.
24. The Spring of Job in Idumaea.
25. A lake in the "Trogodytes."
26. The spring of Siloam.
27. A river in Judaea.
28. Springs in Sardinia.
29. A spring in Epirus.
30. A spring among the Garamantes.

Before detailing the ingenuity with which the VM poet is true to Isidore's original, let us consider instances where he is not. He merges #7 and #9 above (they are, after all, both in Boeothia). He cuts #22 and #23, likewise #26, #27 and #28. Slips of the pen like *Achadia* for Isidore's *Achaia* (line 1223) need no special commentary, but one of his renderings is so outlandish that it fairly jumps off the page: for Isidore's lake *Apuscidamus* he gives lake *Aloe*. How does one get *Aloe* from *Apuscidamus*?

I do not know.

(Duly set off in parentheses, however, I offer a few thoughts. First, Isidore's original:

At contra in Africae lacu Apuscidamo omnia fluitant, nihil mergitur.

["But on the other hand, in Africa's lake Apuscidamus, all things float, nothing sinks."]

The Oxford editor notes that some manuscripts have *alce*, others *alche* instead of *Africae*. If *Africae* is doubtful, then, and if *Apusci-* is a slip of the pen for *Apsuci-* [or, if you prefer, a transposition error], which would give us the Greek word ΑΨΥΧΟΣ [ápsykhos, "without life {psyche}, inanimate"], then one could think that Isidore's original was a Greek description of Israel's *Dead* Sea, where [almost] all things float and [almost] nothing sinks.

If the *VM* poet was working from an *alce* manuscript, and read the *c* as an *o,* then that would account for his *aloe.*

in alce lacu → *in aloe lacu.*

Here endeth the guesswork.)

The *VM* poet *is* a poet, but he finds ways to anchor his fancy to the prose that he is versifying. First, he reuses Isidore's words that have poetic, that is, metrical possibilities: note the last two words of Isidore's sentence.

In Italia fons Ciceronis oculorum vulnera curat.

("In Italy the spring of Cicero cures wounds of the eyes.")

The syllable lengths of *vulnera curat* are long-short-short long-long (metrically, a dactyl and a spondee), which is the trademark rhythm of the last two feet of a dactylic hexameter line. Even in prose, ending a sentence with this kind of metrical swing was an effect the Romans admired: it can be found in the oratory of Cicero and the history of Livy. By the

Middle Ages, judging by its scarcity, the device had lost its "punch," so I suspect that this instance in Isidore is not calculated, but mere coincidence. Be that as it may, however, the *VM* poet seizes on the coincidence; it is a way to minimize the need for poetic jugglery, and allow him to save his creative energies for trickier passages.

Manat in italia fons	Another fountain flows in
alter qui ciceronis	Italy, which is Cicero's,
Dicitur hic oculos ex	It is said; this cures the eyes
omni <u>vulnere curat</u>	from every injury.

Sometimes a little rearranging is necessary. Isidore wrote *Zamae fons in Africa <u>canoras voces</u> facit.*
("The spring at Zama in Africa, makes voices melodious.")
The *VM* poet rearranges the words to compliment the dactylic hexameter line.

Potus dat <u>voces</u> subita	1191.	One drink, and it produces
virtute <u>canoras</u>		melodious voices with sudden power.

An analogous example is found in Isidore's account of springs in Campagna.

In Campania sunt aquae quae sterilitatem feminarum et virorum insaniam abolere dicuntur.
("In Campagna there are waters which are said to do away with the barrenness of women and the madness of men.")

Here, though, the *VM* poet does not avail himself of the metric "tag" that Isidore provides, *(abo)lere dicuntur* (long-short-short long-long), composing instead a "tag" of his own: *(abo)lere virorum.*

Idem dicuntur furias <u>abolere</u> virorum	1201.	The same are said <u>to destroy</u> the furies <u>of men.</u>

On the other hand, the *VM* poet once uses Isidore's original not for the last two feet of a line, but for the first four.

> <u>*In Asphaltite lacu Iudaeae*</u> *nihil mergi potest, quidquid animam habet.*
> ("In the Asphalt lake in Judaea nothing can sink, whatever has a soul.")

<u>*Asphaltite lacu iudee*</u> *corpora mergi*		In the Asphalt lake in Judaea bodies cannot
Nequaquam possunt vegetat dum spiritus illa	1215.	Ever sink while a spirit animates them,

Even thriftier is his versification of Isidore's description of Sicilian springs, the words to be "recycled" being underlined.

> <u>*In Sicilia*</u> <u>*fontes*</u> <u>*sunt*</u> <u>*duo,*</u> *quorum unus* <u>*sterilem*</u> *fecundat,* *alter* <u>*fecundam*</u> *sterilem* <u>*facit*</u>.
> ("In Sicily there are two springs, of which one makes the barren woman fertile, the other makes the fertile woman barren.")

The *VM* poet changes the prepositional phrase *In Sicilia* to the semantically equivalent, but less frequently used locative case (the suffix is *–ae* in classical Latin, *-e* in medieval; the *VM* poet's *sycilie* for *Siciliae* is a perfectly normal medievalization), and, by "finessing" the suffixes, is able to keep the roots "fecund-" and "steril-."

Sunt duo sycilie fontes *steriles facit alter* *Alter fecundans geniali* *lege puellas*	1205.	There are two fountains in Sicily; one makes girls barren, The other making them fertile according to the law of reproduction.

The description of the springs in Campagna, whose prose original we have considered above, is similar.

Qui faciunt steriles *fecundas flumine poto*	1200.	Who make barren women fertile when its stream is drunk.

In one case the *VM* poet is so thrifty that he reuses one of Isidore's words twice.

Cyzici fons amorem Veneris tollit.
("The spring of Cyzicus takes away the love of Venus.)
This becomes *VM* line 1198.

Fons syticus venerem *venerisque repellit* *amorem*	The fountain of Cyzicus drives away libido and the love of sexuality.

More literally, "drives away Venus and the love of Venus."

A charming mini-example of this thriftiness is in the rendering of Isidore's

> *In Indis Siden vocari stagnum, in quo nihil innatat, sed omnia merguntur.*
> ("In India [there is] a pond called Side, in which nothing swims, but everything sinks.")

In the *VM* it begins with an introductory *At contra* ("but on the other hand"). An original touch? No, the phrase is plucked from the following sentence in the original, *at contra in Africae lacu Apuscidamo omnia fluitant, nihil mergitur,* which we have already examined, and grafted onto line 1216.

At contra stagnum syden fert indica tellus	1216.	But on the other hand the soil of India has a pool called Syda,
Quo res nulla natat set mergitur ilico fundo		In which no thing swims, but sinks to the bottom of it.

Further on, Isidore writes:

> *In Aethiopia lacus est quo <u>perfusa</u> corpora velut oleo <u>nitescunt</u>.*
> ("In Ethiopia there is a lake where bodies doused in it shine as if from oil.")

The syllables of *perfusa* are long-long-short; of *nitescunt*, short-long-long. By putting them together, the *VM* poet achieves the metric long-short-short long-long metric "tag" that is the trademark of dactylic hexameter.

Ethiopes etiam stagnum	1188.	They also say that the
perhibentur habere		Ethiopians have a pond
Quo velut ex oleo facies		Which makes the face it is
<u>*perfusa nitescit*</u>		poured on shine as if from oil.

Here, however, we note not only technical ingenuity, but also poetic license: Isidore's lake has become a pond.   There is a metrical reason for this: although both *lacus* and *stagnum* have two syllables, according to the rules of prosody, two consonants together make a short vowel long, so *stagnum* is long-short, while lacus is short-short..   In the same way, when "bodies" become "faces," there are metrical differences because of the lengths of the syllables: *corpora* (because of the consonants *rp*) long-short-short, while *facies* is short-short-long. We see the same mixture of thrift and exuberance in lines 1202-3, which derive from Isidore's

> *In Aethiopiae <u>fonte</u> <u>Rubro</u> <u>qui</u> <u>biberit lymphaticus</u> fit.*
> ("In Ethiopia he who drinks of the Red Spring becomes insane.")

Again underlining the "recycled" words, the *VM* poet has

Ethiopum tellus fert <u>rubro</u>	The soil of the Ethiopians
flumine <u>fontem</u>	contains a fountain with a red current;

Qui <u>bibit</u> ex illo <u>limphaticus</u> *inde redibit*	When a madman drinks from it, thence he will be restored.

The reader will have observed that this passage goes beyond poetic license: it is in fact a rare instance of a mistranslation on the *VM* poet's part: Isidore's drinker becomes insane; in the *VM*, he is restored to his right mind.

Returning to poetic license proper, we find that in line 1221. Isidore's "rocks" become the *VM* poet's "cliff."

In Achaia aqua profluit e saxis Styx appellata, quae ilico potata interficit.
("In Achaia water called Styx flows from the rocks, which, when it is drunk, kills instantly.")

Stix fluuius de rupe fluit *perimet que bibentes*	1221.	The River Styx flows from a cliff and kills those who drink.

Going back to lake Aloe, it is not only rocks that float, but

Omnia set fluitant quamvis *sint plumbea saxa*	But everything floats, even lumps of lead.

Literally, "leaden rocks."

Sometimes, however, a rock is just a rock.
Marsidae fons in Phrygia <u>saxa</u> egerit.
("The spring of Marsidas in Phrygia expels rocks.")

Fons quoque marsidie	1220.	The Marsidian Fountain
compellit <u>saxa</u> natare		also makes rocks swim.

Even when a rock is just a rock, however, making it swim rather than merely being expelled is the mark of the poet.   So is volubility.   Isidore is terse; the *VM* poet is exuberant, and his renderings sometimes overflow the laconic original.   In the case of the "Zama" reference above, the finished product is two lines, not one: this time I have underlined the superfluities.

Affrica fert fontem qui	1190.	Africa has a fountain which
<u>vulgo</u> zama <u>vocatur</u>		<u>is commonly called</u> Zama;
Potus dat voces <u>subita</u>		One drink, and it produces
<u>virtute</u> canoras		melodious voices <u>with</u> <u>sudden power.</u>

Lines 1184-5 are an expansion of a similar prose note. *Nam iuxta Romam Albulae aquae vulneribus medentur.* ("For next to Rome the Albulan waters cure wounds.") *Iuxta Romam* is condensed by a locative, as above, but the two syllables that the *VM* poet saves thereby are immediately "spent" on the gratuitous, if colorful *rapax* ("rushing"), evidently for the alliteration with the preceding *rome*.   *Aquae* ("waters") becomes *amne salubri* ("with a healthful river"); *medentur* ("they heal") expands to *sanare...certo medicamine* ("to heal with sure treatment")

Albula namque rapax	At Rome, for instance, the
rome fluit amne salubri	rushing Albula flows, with its healthful river,

Quem sanare ferunt	1185.	Which, they say, is a sure
certo medicamine vulnus		cure for wounds.

The *VM* poet has selected eleven islands or archipelagoes for description.

1. Thanatos (875-877)
2. The Orkneys (878-80)
3. Thule (881-6)
4. Ireland (887-892)
5. Gades (893-5)
6. The Hesperides (896-7)
7. The Gorgades (898-9)
8. Argire & Crisse (900-901)
9. Ceylon (902-5)
10. Tiles (906-7)
11. The Fortunate Islands (908-915)

There follows a digression on the nine sisters who rule the Fortunate Islands (916-28), and a digression on the passing of Arthur (929-40)

We note again that the *VM* poet is respectful of Isidore, but not slavish: to begin with, he chooses only islands outside the Mediterranean, even though this means ignoring the famous sites that Isidore mentions whose associated history and mythology would seem to tempt his pen.   Also, for no reason that I can see, he changes Isidore's order, reversing the positions of Thule and the Orkneys; he also reverses the order of the "Gorgades" and the Fortunate Isles, although this transposition seems to be purposeful, allowing as it does for the transition to the non-Isidorean material that follows.

These touches are minor, but there is one personal touch in this passage that is of surpassing importance in understanding the *VM*:   the author identifies his nationality.

Insula post nostram	887.	The island after ours that is
prestantior omnibus esse		said to be more excellent

Fertur hibernensis felici	Than all is Ireland, with its
fertilitate	fortunate fertility.

It is reasonable to take this statement of not-Irishness as a statement of Britishness.

Turning our attention to the *VM* itself, we note the trademark latitude of the author in his paraphrases.   Isidore writes *Tanatos insula Oceani freto Gallico, a Brittania aestuario tenui separata* ("Tanatos, an island in the Atlantic separated from Britain by the Gallic Straits [English Channel?], a narrow body of water"); The *VM* poet telescopes this into *adiacet huic* ("it lies near here").   Isidore's *frumentariis campis et gleba uberi* ("with fruitful fields and rich soil") becomes simply *multis rebus* ("with many things").   The *VM* poet is interested in snakes.

Isidore derives Tanatos from *a morte serpentum* ("from the death of snakes"), one assumes, because of its similarity with the Greek word θάνατος ("death"); the *VM* poet at first seems to follow with his Romanization *Thanatos* (θ = th), but his rendering is very free.   There is no Thanatos = death.   Instead, we find an absence: *mortifero serpente caret* ("it lacks a death-dealing snake").

Adiacet huic thanatos que		Nearby lies Thanatos, which
multis rebus habundat		abounds in many things.
Mortifero serpente caret	876.	It lacks a deadly snake, and
tollit que venenum		its soil does away
Si sua cum vino tellus		With venom if it is mixed
commixta bibatur		with wine.

Note that the last line and a half are new.   Isidore's account of Tanatos has nothing about venom at all.

We have observed that the *VM* poet treats the Orkneys next, departing from Isidore's order.   Here is his first statement of his Britishness (my emphases).

Orchades a <u>nobis</u> <u>nostrum</u> *quoque dividit equor*	888.	<u>Our</u> sea divides the Orkneys from <u>us</u>.

We also note an abbreviation: Isidore has *intra Britanniam positae* ("located around Britain").   Afterward, a circumlocution: Isidore's simple *triginta tres* ("thirty-three") becomes the VM's *tres ter dene* ("three thrice-ten"), Isidore's *viginti* ("twenty") becomes *bis dene* ("twice ten"), and instead of Isidore's final *tredecim* ("thirteen"), the *VM* poet gives a perfunctory *alie* ("the others").   Both authors, however, end with the identical verb, *coluntur* ("are farmed").

Hec tres ter dene se iuncto *flumine fiunt*		They are thirty-three in number, divided by the currents.
Bis dene cultore carent *alie que coluntur*	880.	Twenty are untilled, the others are under cultivation.

The description of Thule (*VM*) or Thyle (Isidore) is interesting for its account of the long polar nights and for what I take to be its description of icebergs.   Isidore has *Vnde et pigrum et concretum est eius mare* ("whence its sea is sluggish and solid").   The phrase is echoed by the *VM* poet, who also alludes to the danger that icebergs pose.

Abducit que dies ut	And takes away the days so
semper nocte perhenni	that in the perennial night
Aer agat tenebras faciat 885.	The air always makes
quoque frigore pontum	shadows, it makes the sea freeze
Concretum pigrum que	Solid and sluggish, and at
simul ratibus que negatum	the same time denied to vessels.

Isidore treats Scotland and Ireland as separate islands; the *VM* poet seems to know better, and speaks only of Ireland, and he follows the absence of snakes with the business of Ireland's soil eradicating them. This may be the source of the new material in the "Thanatos" lines. As an example of the *VM* poet's versifying artistry, Isidore's *Illic nulla anguis, avis rara, apis nulla* ("there no snakes, birds few and far between, no bees," my emphases) becomes

Est etenim maior nec apes	It is larger, and produces
nec aves nisi raras	neither bees nor birds except for those seldom encountered,
Educit penitus que negat 891.	And within it does not
generare colubres	allow snakes to reproduce.

Isidore's description of Gades is quite detailed as to geography and etymology of the name; he makes only a passing reference to trees whose sap hardens into gems. The *VM* poet focuses on the gems: he gives them two lines, the geography only one, and transposes Isidore's mention of a dragon, *in quarum hortis fingunt fabulae draconem pervigilem aurea mala servantem* ("in the orchards of which the fables say is a watchful dragon guarding golden apples"), from Isidore's description of the "Gorgades," and inflates Isidore's one line into two.

Gadibus herculeis adiungitur		Gades Island is
insula gades		connected to the Cadiz
		of Hercules.
Nascitur hic arbor cuius de		A tree originates here
cortice gummi		from whose bark a
		gum
Stillat quo gemine fiunt super	895.	Drips, from which
illita iura		gems are made, over
		its broken sap.
Hesperides vigilem perhibentur		They say that the
habere draconem		Hesperides have a
		guardian dragon
Quem servare ferunt sub		Who, they say, keeps
frondibus aurea poma		golden apples under
		leaves.

Isidore's mention of a promontory called *Hesperu Ceras* and hairy women who outrun rabbits are "fingerprints" of the document called *The Circumnavigation of Hanno,* which purports to be an account of a Carthaginian naval expedition around Africa. The details of *Hanno* are beyond the scope of this book, since all that concerns us here is how Isidore, writing more than a millennium after *The Circumnavigation of Hanno* was penned, understood it. He took the text at face value, joining other authors who made *Hanno,* in the happy phrase of the Spanish historian Casariego, *fuente en donde bebieron los geógrafos grecolatinos* ("a fountain where the Greco-Roman geographers drank"),[11] for all its strangeness and ambiguity.

In his versification of Isidore's account of the other islands, Chryse, Argyre, Ceylon and Tiles, the VM poet is quite workmanlike, and consistent with the palette that we have observed. Then, abruptly, he leaves Isidore behind with his description of the Fortunate Isles, transposed from its place before the "Gorgades," and transposed as well into the imagery of the Celtic Otherworld: the islands are ruled by thrice-three sisters with magical powers, to whom Arthur is brought to be healed of his wounds.   It will be noted that the narrative changes from the impersonal to "we."   I am unable to identify an antecedent for this episode.   Normally it would be bad form to end a chapter on a note of puzzlement, but since this chapter is about an anonymous versification of Isidore of Seville, and since we have left Isidore behind, we may treat this puzzlement as an incentive for future research.

---

[11] Casariego 7.

Quasi-Anonymity:

Hrotsvit of Gandersheim's *Pelagius*

Back in 1864, the author of *Shakespeare in Germany* began his study by establishing a benchmark, not with the dramas of Goethe and Schiller, but with the Latin plays "which the learned nun Hrotsvita composed in the tenth century in the nunnery of Gandersheim, in the Hartz mountains."[1]   His point was that there is a great dearth of good theater in Germany between the time of Hrotsvit (as she is commonly known at the beginning of the twenty-first century) and the age of Goethe and Schiller.   The author adds a parenthetical observation that Hrotsvit's plays "contain among numerous traces of their genuine Germanic Saxon origin, many passages which remind one strongly of Shakespeare," and he backs this claim up with a page-long list of parallel passages between Hrotsvit and The Bard.[2]   Well and good: the touches that make theater effective are noteworthy regardless of their source.   There is a disparity of genre, however, since drama is a far smaller proportion of Hrotsvit's output than Shakespeare's: most of her work is in the genre of the long poem, or short epic, if you will, as opposed to the epic proper of Virgil and Homer.

---

[1]   Cohn I.
[2]   Cohn I-II.

Pelagius, the verse narrative by Hrotsvit of Gandersheim, is of particular relevance to this book because it is an example of literary excellence that is, as will be demonstrated, to all intents and purposes anonymous.   Apart from its excellence in the abstract, however, it is important for its place in the western literary continuum, because it is one of the earliest portrayals of Moslem society to a Northern European audience.   A portrayal is necessarily subjective, and comparison of this fantasy (in the sense of a work of imagination) with objective historical knowns will provide insights to the author's mind.   The setting is Cordoba; the subject is the martyrdom of the boy Pelagius. Here is a line and section overview:

(1-11) Invocation.

(12-90) Cordoba.   Its Christian past, its sufferings under its non-Christian conquerors, a portrayal of the despotic king "Abdrahemen."

(91-178) Galicia.   Abdrahemen is incensed by its freedom, and leads an expedition against it; Galicia's prince and twelve counts are captured.   The prince's handsome son, Pelagius, takes his father's place as a hostage.

(179-187) Interlude.   The Moslems are God's chastisement.

(188-217) Back in Cordoba. Pelagius is put into prison. Cordoban civic leaders intend to use him as a pawn: the king is a homosexual, and they hope that Pelagius's good looks will translate into influence at court.

(218-275) The palace.   Abdrahemen is indeed "hot" for Pelagius, but when he attempts to force a kiss on him, the young man punches him in the mouth, drawing blood.

(276-297) Punishment. Abdrahemen orders Pelagius to be shot from a catapult, but to no effect; instead, he orders Pelagius beheaded.

(298-413) Sainthood.   Pelagius's body is located and enshrined, is found efficacious for cures, and is successfully tested for saintliness.

In the epilogue to the first part of her works[3] Hrotsvit writes that she got the material for her saints' lives from old books,

> *excepta superius scripta passione sancti Pelagii · Cuius seriem martirii quidam eiusdem in qua passus est indigena civitatis mihi exposuit · qui ipsum pulcherrimum virorum se vidisse et exitum rei attestatus est veraciter agnovisse · Unde si quid in utroque falsitatis dictando comprehendi · non ex meo fefelli sed fallentes incaute imitate fui ·*

> ("...except for the   suffering of St. Pelagius, written above. A certain inhabitant of the city in which the events of his martyrdom transpired, told me that he had seen that most handsome of men himself, and was a witness to the outcome of the matter, and knew it truly.   From which if in [my] account of either [event] I have included anything false, I have not done the falsifying, but have unwittingly followed falsifiers.")

I take Hrotsvit at her word.   She must have had an informed source, whether or not Spanish documents were available to her, since her version of the events does not agree with any known text from Spain.   Modern anthologist McMillin writes,

> It is highly unlikely that Hrotsvit would have had any access to the Spanish accounts of Pelagius's martyrdom, in

---

[3]   Berschin 131.

either the saint's life [of the Spaniard Raguel, author of the earliest known account] or the Mozarabic liturgy.   There is no evidence that these texts traveled north of the Pyrenees until well after the tenth century.   Indeed, Hrotsvit and Raguel disagree on a variety of details of the saint's story.   In Hrotsvit, Pelagius serves as hostage in place of his father rather than an uncle, is shot from a catapult, is beheaded rather than hacked to death, and undergoes a variety of postmortem tests to prove his sanctity rather than being instantly canonized.[4]

We can accept Hrotsvit's statement, but let us not stretch it too thin.   The fact remains that much of what she wrote in *Pelagius* does not match what we know of Islam or of history.   Did she in fact follow a falsifier, an informant who garbled the facts? Did she have a reliable informant, but misinterpreted details of his account as the result of honest misunderstanding?   Was she writing propaganda?   We will never know the reason for the discrepancies and omissions in *Pelagius*, but it is worthwhile to examine them, as we shall do in due course.

First things first, however.   It is important to acknowledge at the outset how little is known of this Hrotsvit of Gandersheim. There is a Gandersheim, located in central Germany, and there was an abbey founded there in 852;[5] Hrotsvit repeatedly addresses a mentor named Gerberg, and Gandersheim had two abbesses of that name.   Beyond this, however, the details of our author's biography are only those that can be inferred from her

---

[4]   McMillin 41.
[5]   St. John, viii.

works and cross-checked with history: for example, she speaks of Gerberg as *aetate minor* ("younger in age"),[6] and since Gerberg II was born *ca.*940, this gives us a reference point for Hrotsvit's birth. Since this same Gerberg was the niece of Holy Roman Emperor Otto I, we can infer that Hrotsvit had connections at court.

The rest is unknown. This is not surprising: self-effacement was the norm in the monastic orders in the Middle Ages, as in the phrase a*ma nesciri* ("love to be unknown"). Her very name is uncertain: in older scholarship she was known as Hroswitha, Rotsuith and Hrosvita (which is close to the spelling we find in the prologue to *Pelagius*, "Hrotsvitha[m]," and on three other occasions[7] as well); and an Internet search reveals that she is remembered as Roswitha in modern-day Gandersheim, which has a Roswitha Clinic and statuary dedicated to "the first German poetess" at the Roswitha Fountain. When I was introduced to her work in days gone by she was "Roswitha," too. I now call her "Hrotsvit" not because that form is demonstrably more accurate (it occurs only twice[8] in the index to her collected works), but because "Hrotsvit" is the name that the current scholarly consensus has gravitated to, and I gravitate with it.

I do draw the line, however, at accepting the current scholarly consensus as to the etymology of her name. True, some of the derivations that had been proposed were fanciful: *Weiße Rose* ("white rose"), *Rascher Wind* ("fast wind") or *Roß- Rosenweide* ("horse-" "rose-meadow").[9] The proposal

---

[6] Berschin 2.
[7] *Maria* 18, *Ascension* 148 and *Gong* 12.
[8] Hrotsvit 134.3, 271.3.
[9] Hrotsvit 5.

now in fashion, however, is more than merely fanciful: "mighty voice of Gandersheim" is not only wishful thinking, but mistranslation.   True, Hrotsvit does write — once — that she is *clamor validus Gandeshemensis*.[10] This is nowadays interpreted to be a Latinization of her name, but there is no evidence that this is so, despite modern scholars' owlish attempts to nudge the reader in that direction by capitalization (*Clamor Validus*).   On the contrary, it is when understood literally that the words fit their context better: our author is contrasting herself with the Roman playwright Terence, who is said to appeal to readers *dulcedine sermonis* ("by the sweetness of his speech").   *Clamor* is not "voice" (that would be *vox*), but "uproar, din;" nor does *validus* correspond to "mighty" (as in *potens*), but "hale," as Hrotsvit herself uses the word (twice) in *Pelagius*:   *Quam crebro validę cepit luctamine pugne* ("which [city] he had seized [only] after repeated efforts and strenuous fighting," 49) and *Ast ego sed validis dominabor quippe lacertis* ("but I, with [my] brawny arms, will surely master," 156).   Thus, in contrast to "sweet-speeched" Terence, she describes herself as Gandersheim's "hearty noise," which, as we shall see, is a perfect description of her plays, which abound in slapstick and outrageous dialogue.

I remember my chagrin when I discovered Hrotsvit, at the wasted years of dutifully plodding through truly boring Latin authors, that I could have spent getting to know this lively, opinionated, outspoken lady.   I was fortunate, however, to have discovered her directly, on the page, because the critical literature about her, which I came across later, too late to spoil

---

[10] Berschin 132.

her for me, has produced more smoke than light. Mid-twentieth century "crit" approached her with the preconception that, since she was religious, her work must, *ipso facto,* be humorless. A corrective view was proposed by Peter Dronke in a chapter in his 1984 book: he even described Hrotsvit as "coquettish," which was a step in the right direction, but spoiled his argument by announcing that in her prefaces, "she says little of what she really means and means nothing of what she says."[11] This doesn't leave the rest of us much to work with, and we may be curious as to the source of Dronke's omniscience in this particular matter, but his study is otherwise stimulating, not only as a corrective of the presupposition that Hrotsvit was humorless, but also of the mainstream's sins of omission, that her work contains no personal elements and that it makes no reference to the celebrities of her day. Dronke's attempt to lighten things up had no cheering effect on subsequent writers, who continued to produce ponderous analyses of passages that are clearly laugh-provoking: in the play *Sapientia* ("wisdom," the name of the heroine), the villain's question "How old are your daughters?" is answered by Sapientia with a farrago of mathematical jargon. The shtick of the leading lady rattling off equations while the Bad Guy sits open-mouthed, is the sort of scene that brings out the ham in actors. We cannot know if the scene is an inside joke, a "dig" at a court mathematician, perhaps, but we can infer that the scene got a big laugh when performed at a girls' night "out" at Gandersheim, since Hrotsvit inserts the same shtick of reeling off learnèd mumbo-jumbo (musicology, in this case) in another play, *Paphnutius.* I

---

[11] Dronke 69.

suspect that it would still get a laugh today, if played as it is on the page, without preconceptions.

A late twentieth century variation of Hrotsvit-as-humorless is Hrotsvit-as-bookish. A passage in a recent book by Tolan speaks of "Sabaean frankincense (which Hrotsvitha associates with Arabs thanks to her reading of Isidore)." [12] The encyclopedist Isidore of Seville was indeed widely read in the middle ages, but if Hrotsvit knew him, her acquaintance would seem to have been limited to the two passages that Tolan cites.

Instead of portraying her as a pinpoint Isidorean, it is much more fruitful to refer to the pervasive influence of Virgil. Hrotsvit's phrase *ture Sabeo* ("incense of Sabah," frankincense, 66) is a Virgilian echo (as in *Aeneid* 1.146 and *Georgics* 2.117), as is *vela dabant* ("they set sail," 327), which recalls the well-known passage in the *Aeneid* that sets up the storm at sea [1.35]), and *belloque superbam* ("haughty in war," 93, referring to Galicia; Virgil applies it to Rome in *Aeneid* 1.21) as are turns of phrase like *miserabile dictum* ("sadly said"), which would seem to be a subtle modification of Virgil's *mirabile dictu* ("wondrous to relate"), and his speaking of Carthage as *Tyrii tenuere coloni* ("Tyrian inhabitants held [it], *Aeneid* 1.12) would seem to have found echoes in *Pelagius: Hispanii...tenuere coloni* ("Hispanic inhabitants held [it], 14), *duros huiusce colonos* ("tough inhabitants of that city," 25) and *Paganos iustis intermiscendo colonis* ("by mixing pagans with the just inhabitants"). More instructive, however, is a close look at the following lines, from the passage where young Pelagius is being showered with kisses by the homosexual Abdrahemen.

---

[12] Tolan 106.

Fronteque summisso libaverat oscula caro / Affectus causa complectens utpote colla ("and with his forehead low he showered kisses on the dear boy, / being excited, as you might expect, embracing his neck," 237). *Colla*? But the word is should be *collum* ("neck"). *Colla* is "necks." Four lines later, Pelagius disdains Abdrahemen's advances, *Magno ridiculo divertens ora negata* ("with great mockery turning away the mouth he was denying"). The word for mouth is *os*; *ora* is the plural. Plural for singular is a Virgilian vice: he will write *vox faucibus haesit* ("[my] voice stuck in [my] throats"), because he wrote in dactylic hexameter, the meter *par excellence* of epic poetry, which consists of six beats per line, the syllables of each beat being either long-short-short (a dactyl) or long-long (a spondee). Latin has too many long syllables for this to be a natural rhythm, so Latin authors "fudge" in a variety of ways. Virgil's way of fudging, plural for singular, is so pervasive that the reader forgets that it is there; I confess that I read right over the three times (by my count) that Hrotsvit fudges this way, not noticing it until my third close reading of *Pelagius.* It is noteworthy and praiseworthy that Hrotsvit usually faces metrical difficulties squarely, relying on filler words like *denique* ("then") and *corpora* ("bodies") rather than on dodges that do violence to meaning. The passages that I have cited indicate artistic integrity: she knew of this Virgilian way of cutting corners but, except as noted, declined to avail herself of it.

It is odd that Statius, also widely read in the middle ages, has never been proposed as a literary antecedent of Hrotsvit. During my first close reading of *Pelagius* I had noticed an unusually high frequency of compound adjectives and nouns. Compounds of this sort are not common in Latin literature; the following are not in the *Oxford Latin Dictionary*, and so may be Hrotsvit's original coinages: *altithroni* ("high-throned," 93) and *grandisonas* ("big-sounding," 325), both on the analogy of the more common *altisonus* ("deep-sounding"), *celsithronum* ("high-throned," 374), and *flammivomis* ("flame-spewing," 400). The *O.L.D.* does have *fluctivagos* ("wave-wandering," 323), matching three passages in Statius's *Thebaid* (1.271, 9.305 and 9.360) and one in his *Silvae* (3.I.84); if two occurrences are enough to make Hrotsvit a pinpoint Isidorean, then four should make her a pinpoint Statian. I leave that line of inquiry to someone else, not only because Statius's rant is not my cup of tea, but because the two poets have practically nothing in common; it is more fruitful to consider these compound words as being natural to a German speaker, which we may assume that Hrotsvit was.

(Although whether German was her first or second language is an open question, given the cosmopolitan nature of the times. Compounds are also idiomatic in Dutch, and if we take the similarity between the homonyms *Hrots-* and *groots* ("grand") as a fingerprint, then it might be that Hrotsvit was the first Dutch poetess.)

At the turn of the twenty-first century the assumption became widespread that the Roman dramatist Terence was Hrotsvit's literary model; if true, it would make her useless as a commentator on Moorish Spain, since Terence's plays are abstract, out of space and time, consisting of stock characters and fortune-cookie dialogue. Writers at the turn of the twentieth century, much wiser than we in matters of Latinity, had rejected the connection outright. The Terentian hypothesis was advanced by argumentation that was frequently tortuous and sometimes New Age; it proceeded from assumptions based on a misreading of the already-misread *"clamor validus"* passage.

> *Sunt etiam alii sacris inherentes paginis · qui licet alia gentilium spernant · Terentii tamen fingmenta frequentius lectitant · et dum dulcedine sermonis delectantur · nefandarum notitia rerum maculantur · Unde ego clamor validus* (my non-caps) *Gandeshemensis · non recusavi illum imitari dictando · dum alii colunt legendo · quo eodem dictationis genere · quo turpia lascivarum incesta feminarum recitabantur · laudabilis sacrarum castimonia virginum iuxta mei facultatem ingenioli celebraretur ·*[13]
>
> ("For there are others, cleaving to sacred pages, who rightly reject heathens' other works, still quite frequently read the concoctions of Terence, and while they are pleased with the sweetness of his speech, they are stained with a story of sordid matters. From which I, the hearty noise of Gandersheim, have not shrunk from imitating him in composing, while others venerate [him] by reading. By which, in the same genre of composition [*dictationis genere*] in which foul promiscuities of sluts are recounted, with the help of my little muse the praiseworthy chastity of holy virgins is extolled.")

Dronke cites contemporary biography in which Bruno, the emperor's brother (and therefore Gerberg's uncle), is said to have interspersed his wide reading with risqué theatrical works,

---

[13] Berschin 132.

not for their ribaldry, we are assured, but for their elegant style.[14]
If so, Hrotsvit would seem to have been skeptical of the motives
of Bruno's grammar-quest, and this passage could be a dig at
this palace celebrity.

Be that as it may, when we take Hrotsvit's words at face
value, we see that the only similarity with Terence that she
claims is genre: Terence wrote for the stage, I write for the
stage.   Everything else in this passage is contrastive.   If it
needs to be said again, I will say it again: Hrotsvit is not in the
Terentian tradition, either in poetic technique, subject matter,
tempo, tone or, most importantly, theatricality.   A play is not a
play until it is performed.   We must accordingly use our mind's
eye as we read, to imagine how the play looks onstage.
Terence's comedies are all chit-chat; Hrotsvit's plays *move*.

Hrotsvit's theatrical soul-mate is madcap Plautus.   I do not
know whether the relationship between the two playwrights is
the result of her reading or merely a coincidence of temperament,
but it is evident that both share a love of verbal razzle-dazzle.
Note the Plautine diminutives that pour from a frantic Emperor
Hadrian: [15]   *O iniuria · quod a tantilla etiam contempnor*
homullula · ("This is outrageous!   I'm being insulted by this
little... this munchkin!").   They also share a love of Chaplinesque
sight-gags.   Consider the farcical tone, the "hearty noise," of the
first of three martyrdoms in *Sapientia*; at the order of Emperor
Hadrian, who Hrotsvit portrays as out-Heroding Herod,
Sapientia's daughter Fides ("faith"), consistently saucy through
being flogged (the floggers get tired) and having had her nipples

---

[14] Dronke 57.
[15] Berschin 262.

cut off (milk came out), is being roasted on a gridiron. The jingle-jangle of rhyme makes Hadrian's threats sound ridiculous, and Fides's mockery all the saucier.

FIDES · *...unde commodę pauso in craticula · ceu in tranquilla navicula ·*

ADRIANUS · *Sartago plena pice et cęra ardentibus rogis superponatur · et in ferventem liquorem haec rebellis mittatur*

FIDES · Sponte insilio ·

ADRIANUS · *Consentio ·*

FIDES · *Ubi sunt minę tuę? ecce illesa · inter ferventem liquorem ludens nato · et pro vi caumatis · sentio matutini refrigerium roris ·*

ADRIANUS · Antioche quid ad hec est agendum?

ANTIOCHUS · *Ne evadat providendum ·*

ADRIANUS · *Capite truncetur ·*

ANTIOCHUS · *Alioquin non vincetur ·* [16]

("Fides: ...from which I relax on this gridiron as if it were a lazily drifting canoe.

Hadrian: A cauldron full of tar and wax! Put it over a blazing fire! Then throw this obnoxious girl into the boiling liquid!

Fides: I hop in of my own free will.

Hadrian: That's fine with me!

Fides: Where are your threats? Look, unharmed I playfully swim amid your "boiling liquid," and its fierce heat seems as cooling as the morning dew.

---

[16] Berschin 156-7.

> Hadrian: Antiochus, what do we do or say?
> Antiochus: Make sure she can't get away.
> Hadrian: Off with her head, I guess.
> Antiochus: Otherwise, no success.")

It is crucial that we understand the comedic side of Hrosvit's talent in order to appreciate the deadly seriousness of the martyrdom scene in *Pelagius.*

From authorial matters we return to questions of plot, as outlined at the opening of this essay.   The reader may be struck by the loose ends in Hrotsvit's story: what happens to Pelagius's father?   What happens to Abdrahemen?   Who are the Cordobans who propose Pelagius for the palace "guard?" Recent scholarship takes it as a given that they are kindly but godless Moslems, but Hrotsvit does not say so; she says *Illic ergo viri venerunt sedulo primi / Mulcendo mentem iuvenis causa pietatis* ("then the first men, concerned, came   / for soothing the mind of   the young man out of kindliness"). They might just as well be Christians made cynical and corrupt by oppression.   The same question could be asked of the fishermen who discover Pelagius's body, but despite the assumptions of the moderns (that they are Moslems intent only on reward money), Hrotsvit does not say.   We will touch on other episodes in the tale besides these four where Hrotsvit passes up material that would seem to make for good poetry. Normally, our author is never in a rush: in her plays she regularly *protracts* the shtick, and in the epic *Gesta Ottonis* ("Deeds of Otto"), when she deals with the delicate question of the treason of the emperor's brother Henry, who also happened to be the father of her benefactress Gerberg, her writing is remarkable for its leisurely tact. My interpretation of the streamlining in *Pelagius* (the poetess is unavailable for comment) is that Hrotsvit stripped her tale of anything that would impede its momentum or distract from its focus, to make her story as hard-hitting as possible.

Such details as are included, then, are included for a reason, and deserve a close look both as internals in a literary work, and in the context of historical externals. Let us begin by considering both at the same time, with the name Hrotsvit gave to the king of Cordoba.

From a literary point of view, it suffices to say that Abdrahemen is dactylic. *Pelagius* is written in dactylic hexameter, as we have noted; by the rules of prosody, the first three syllables of Abd-ra-he-men are long-short-short, and the last one is ambiguous. The name, then, fits the meter, and therefore was a good choice.

It was a choice that must have made Otto's diplomats wince, however. Negotiations with Abd ar-Rahman III, the caliph of Cordoba, had been long and difficult: the Moorish monarch's opening gambit had been to detain the German ambassador for *three years* because a letter of introduction was allegedly disrespectful to Mohammed. According to the ambassador's biographer, a Jewish intermediary named Hasdeu had warned him of how touchy the caliph could be.

"Periculosum", inquit Judaeus, "cum hac regem videre. Cauti certe sitis, quit nuntiis vobis missis regi responedeatis. Legis enim severitatem iam vobis innotuisse non dubito, eique declinandae prudenter oportet consulere."

("[It's] dangerous," said the Jew, "to see the king with this [letter]. The emissaries having been sent to you, you should certainly be careful how you answer the king. Now, I don't doubt that you have noted the severity of the law, and you'll have to be sensitive about [the way] it is read to him.")[17]

Memories of this wearying, although ultimately successful, ordeal must have still lingered at the Ottonian court; how the statesmen must have shuddered at the thought of having to go back to square one, their efforts annulled by caliphal pique should it become known that an epic had appeared in which a Moorish king is mocked as a pederast, and who is humiliated by an infidel who is a mere boy!

(The reason for this embassy is not clear. It is common nowadays to assume that its purpose was to protest the activities of Moslem pirates operating out of the Mediterranean port of Fraxinetum, but there are two other possibilities: Fraxinetum had provided safe haven for Adalbert, a rebel against Otto I,[18] and so the motive may have been some sort of extradition treaty; a more prosaic explanation may be that the German mission, sent in 953, was nothing more than reactive, a pro forma reflex to the mission sent by the Byzantines in 949.[19] Cordoba received another Byzantine delegation in 972; coincidentally or not, Otto II sent ambassadors in 974.[20])

---

[17] Vazquez de Parga 74.
[18] Hill 138.
[19] O'Callaghan 119.
[20] O'Callaghan 125.

Abdrahemen /Abd ar-Rahman is not the only instance where we can profitably compare externals and internals: Abdrahemen attacks Galicia, the Christian kingdom in northwest Spain; on July 26th of the year 920 Abd ar-Rahman III defeated a Christian army of Galicians and Pamplonans at Valdejunquera, in northern Spain.[21] "Pelagius" corresponds to "Pelayo," the name of the young Spanish martyr.[22] These historical nuggets give the narrative credibility.

Most correspondences, however, are not nuggets, but ore that needs refining. Hrotsvit portrays Abd ar-Rahman III as commanding an invincible war machine, but in fact the caliph was not always as successful as he was at Valdejunquera; his armies were defeated by King Ramiro II of León in 933 and again in 939. On the latter occasion the caliph was personally in command; he took out his frustration at being defeated by crucifying three hundred of his followers.[23] I cannot imagine Hrotsvit passing up a lurid episode like this, so its absence from *Pelagius* is evidence that her knowledge of the status quo in Spain was sketchy, or, if you will, impressionistic rather than detailed.

Abd ar-Rahman III allowed the Christians of Cordoba to practice their religion,[24] and many of them found the status quo bearable, as witness a certain Cordoban bishop who attempted to persuade the excitable Ottonian ambassador not to rock the boat.

---

[21] O'Callaghan 122.
[22] Fletcher 57.
[23] O'Callaghan 122.
[24] O'Callaghan 117.

"Considerate', ait, 'sub qua conditione agamus.   Peccatis ad haec devoluti sumus, ut paganorum subiaceamus ditioni."
("Consider," he said, "under what condition[s] we must proceed.   We are brought low by our sins, so that we must lie under the sway of pagans.")

The reader will recall from the opening synopsis that Hrotsvit makes the same point: the Moslems triumph not because of their superiority, *Sed mage iudicio secreti iudicis aequo / Ut populus tanto correptus rite flagello / Fleret totius proprii commissa reatus* ("but rather from the just sentence of the secret Judge, so that the people, duly afflicted with such a scourge, [when] accused, might bewail all [the sins] that they have committed," 181-3).   The bishop continues.

Resistere potestati verbo prohibemur apostoli.   Tantum hoc unum relictum est solatii, quod in tantae clamitatis malo legibus nos propriis uti non prohibent; qui quos diligentes christianitatis viderint observatores, colunt et amplectuntur, simul ipsorum convictu delectantur, cum Iudaeos penitus exhorreant.   Pro tempore igitur hoc videmur tenere consilio, ut quia religionis nulla infertur iactura, cetera eis obsequamur, iussisque eorum in quantum fidem non impediunt obtemperemus.[25]
("We are forbidden to resist authority by the word of the apostle.   The only consolation we have in the evil of such a great calamity is that they do not prevent us from using our own laws;   they see that we are sincere in our

---

[25]   Vazquez de Parga 75.

Christianity, and they treat us well and include us, in the same way that they enjoy the company of their co-religionists, while they loathe the Jews from the bottom of their hearts. For the time being, therefore, it seems [best] to us to have the following policy: as long as there is no interference with our religion, we obey their other commands, and we put up with their orders that do not hinder the faith.")

The picture, then, is of a *modus vivendi* of making the best of a bad situation. The ambassador saw things differently.

Johannes paulum commotior: 'Alium', inquit 'quam te, qui videris episcopus, haec proferre decuerat. Cum sis enim fidei assertor, eiusque te gradus celsior posuerit etiam defensorem, timore humano a veritate praedicanda necdum alios compescere, sed nec te ipsum oportebat subducere; et melius omnino fuerat, hominem christianum famis grave ferre dispendium, quam cibis ad destructionem aliorum consociari gentilium.[26]

("John [the ambassador] said, a bit heatedly, 'It would have been more fitting for this to come from someone other than you, who seem to be a bishop. Since you are supposed to be a proclaimer of the faith, and your higher rank will have made you its defender, you should not because of human fear hold others back from preaching the truth, nor should you yourself shrink from doing it; and it would be better for a Christian to suffer dire hunger than to attend the banquets

---

[26] Smith 65.

of foreigners [which lead] to [his] destruction [or: banquets of pagans that lead to the destruction of others].")

There were Cordobans who agreed with the ambassador, chafing under what Hrotsvit calls a *simulata pace* ("simulated peace," 61), and actually courted martyrdom by publicly slanging the Moslems' faith, as other contemporary documents attest.

> *Sunt autem plerique fidelium, et, heu proh dolor, etiam sacerdotorum, temere horum confessorum gloriam adimere non verentes, qui iubent eos non recipi in catalogo sanctorum, inusitatum scilicet, atque prophanum asserentes huiusmodi martyrium.*[27]
> ("There are, however, many of the faithful, and, alas, even of the priesthood, thoughtlessly, without revering the glory of those witnesses, who order them not to be received in the catalogue of saints, pushing for a martyrdom of a sort that is clearly bizarre and profane.")

Hrotsvit describes them more flatteringly: *Sed si quos ignis Christi succensit amoris, / Martiriique sitis suasit corrumpere dictis / Marmora... / Hos capitis subito damnavit denique poena: / Sed superos anime petierunt sanguine lotę.* ("But if the fire of the love of Christ inflamed them, and the thirst for martyrdom urged them to vilify the marble [idols] by [their] speech...then [the caliph] immediately sentenced these to death: but the souls washed in blood sought [realms] above," 63-5, 67-8). McMillin correctly identifies the author's "spin:"

---

[27] Vazquez de Parga 67.

"Given Islamic law, Christian martyrdom in Cordoba was not automatic, not a matter of simply being faithful to Christianity. Rather, to be martyred, one had to go out of one's way to publicly insult Islam."[28]   The official opinion, however, was that this kind of martyrdom was gratuitous and narcissistic (*superbia,* below, is much stronger, less ambiguous than our "pride."). *Quippe quos nulla violentia praesidalis fidem suam negare compulit, nec a cultu sanctae piaeque religionis amouit, sed propria se voluntate discrimini offerentes, ob superbiam suam...* ("Indeed no governmental violence compels them to deny their faith, nor removes them from following pure and holy religion, but voluntarily offering themselves to judgment, on account of their narcissism..."). The document closes with reminders that a Christian is supposed to love his enemies, return good for evil, and refrain from wicked talk, all of which would prohibit the faithful from "entrapping" Moslems to commit the sin of murder. Hrotsvit's sympathy for these quixotic souls notwithstanding, Pelagius does not support their point of view.

> Hrotsvit is careful to present Pelagius's tale in such a way a to distance him from these earlier martyrs as well. He is an outsider, not a local resident. He goes to Cordoba in order to spare his father, not to seek martyrdom actively. He is passive and silent both in prison and when first brought to court. His insult to Islam comes only under duress, after he is physically embraced by the king.[29]

---

[28] McMillin 49.
[29] McMillin 50.

All of the above misses the very important point, however, that the Christians are in no way singled out, as is made plain is the report of Otto's delegation.

> *Eis in legibus primum dirumque est, ne quis in religionem eorum quid umquam audeat loqui. Civis sit, extraneus sit, nulla intercedente redemptione capite plectitur. Si rex ipse audierit et in crastinum gladium retinuerit, ipse morti adducitur, nec ulla intervenire potest clementia.*[30]
> ("In those laws the first and most drastic is that no one may dare to speak anything at all against their religion. Whether a citizen or an alien, he is beheaded without any clemency. If the king himself heard, and withheld his sword until the next day, he himself would be led off to death, without any intervening clemency being possible.")

We are getting ahead of ourselves, however. For now, suffice it to say that the historical Cordoban Christians were allowed to practice their religion.

In *Pelagius,* Abdrahemen's predecessors do so out of avarice. "...Hrotsvit sees the motivation for this decree is to be greed rather than tolerance. Her judgment is not without merit — Islamic rulers could not tax fellow Muslims. Therefore, Christians and Jews were an important part of the tax base throughout the Islamic world."[31] McMillin is historically correct, but the only way our author would have known this is

---

[30] Vazquez de Parga 72.
[31] McMillin 49.

from an informed source, which again supports her statement that she worked from an eyewitness account.

Hrotsvit's Abdrahemen, however, is *Deterior patribus* ("worse than his [fore]fathers") in that he too fierce to be bought off. His *superbia* is greater than his greed. He permits a similar religious toleration, but only up to the edge of town. *Sepius innocuo madefecit sanguine rura / Corpora iustorum consumens sancta virorum* ("He quite often drenched the countryside with innocent blood, consuming saintly bodies of just men.") In Cordoba he is represented as tolerant only because he is backing down before the determined resistance of the Christians, who can only be pushed so far: *Dicens malle mori, legem quoque morte tueri, / Vivere quam stulte, sacris famulando novellis* ("Saying that [the Christian community] would prefer to die, even to face the death penalty / rather than live foolishly serving outlandish rituals"). Abdrahemen is cruel as well: he doubles the ransom for Pelagius's father precisely so that it cannot be paid: *Non sitiens tantum precii, quod defuit, aurum, / Quantum rectorem populi gestit dare morti* ("not thirsting for the value of so much gold, which was lacking, as he worked to put the leader of the people to death," 141-2).

Historically, indifference to ransom would be quite out of character for any medieval ruler, since the expense of a military campaign was partly defrayed by booty.[32] The portrayal of the Moorish king as a fire-breathing fanatic is contradicted by the chronicle of the German embassy. *Rex undique meticulosus ancepsque, periculum sibi posse imminere considerans, artibus*

---

[32] Fletcher 57.

omnis generis quo evadat pertemptat ("The caliph was always jittery and indecisive, obsessing about possible danger to himself, [and] he made use of all sorts of tricks to avoid it"). He tried carrot-and-stick psychological warfare against the ambassador, but when that tough-minded monk was not intimidated, it was the caliph that extended the olive branch.

History records that Abd ar-Rahman III declared his independence from the rest of Islam on January 16, 929,[33] adopting the title "caliph." Evidently, however, "caliph" was explained to Hrotsvit in terms that scandalized her: true, a caliph is a greater king than other, petty kings, but if someone, trying to be helpful, defined the title for her as *rex regum* ("king of kings"), it was an unfortunate definition. The only other time that I know of in Hrotsvit's works that she uses this title is in the first line of *Gesta Ottonis,* where she is referring to God Almighty. When she uses it with Abdrahemen, she does so with a sneer. She writes *Ut regem regum semet fore <u>crederet</u> ipsum* ("so that he <u>believed</u> that he was the King of Kings," 87, my emphasis): not that he *proclaimed* himself king of kings, but that he *believed* that he was, which would indicate delusional megalomania.

(Stephen L. Wailes has presented a "softer" interpretation, in the "Hrotsvit-as-bookish" tradition. He correctly cites passages in the Old Testament where the phrase "king of kings" is used with the despots Artaxerxes and Nebuchadnezzar. "Aligning him with those heathens in arrogant pretension to a divine name, Hrotsvit writes large the spiritual sin of pride in Abdrahemen, which fuels his lust for conquest and

---

[33] O'Callaghan 118.

domination."[34]   I disagree, because I cannot imagine the "hearty noise of Gandersheim" writing anything so subtle, so roundabout, so recherché.   Hrotsvit's poetry is forceful, not recherché.)

Hrotsvit does not tell us that the historical Abd ar-Rahman's mother was Frankish, a *rumiyya* ("Roman," that is, a Christian[35]), that his grandmother was Basque, that he became king at age 20 (in the year 912), and that he had a fifty-year reign,[36] all of which would seem to have been the sort of material that makes for interesting poetry.   Another omission involves a crucial element of the cultural background: except for the name Abdrahemen, I am unable to find anything in the poem that is recognizable as Arabic or Moslem at all.   There is not even a reference to Mecca.

On the contrary, the historically monotheistic Moslems are expressly portrayed as polytheistic idolaters, *diis auro fabricatis* ("with gods made of gold," 57).   Their gods are *marmora* ("marble [statues]," 65), said to be *stultos divos* ("stupid gods," 84) and as an impeccably classical touch, are worshipped *cespite* ("on [a] turf [altar]," 248), in the Roman mode.

History is silent on the private life of Abd ar-Rahman III. As for Abdrahemen's pederasty, two prefatory points need to be made.   First, although Hrotsvit portrays a predatory homosexual in *Pelagius,* her other villains are predatory heterosexuals: true, it is not often in medieval literature that we find a man exclaiming *O lascive puer* ("oh, you sexy boy," 250), but Hrotsvit has the phrase *lascivae puelle* ("sexy girls") twice in the

---

[34] Wailes 69.
[35] Fierro 38.
[36] McMillin 51.

play *Dulcitius.*[37]   Comparison with the desperate, flustered villains in the plays will also show that there is not much difference between their dialogue and that of Abdrahemen. The second point is that modern scholarship breaks down completely on this issue, since it is fixated on the New Age question of how a writer as cool as Hrotsvit could be so un-cool on the subject of homosexuality.   Yet un-cool she was: throughout her works she praises virginity, which is not easy to reconcile with sodomy; but neither is it easy to reconcile with free-and-easy New Age promiscuity.   Let us take Hrotsvit at her word: she was a "square," and when she says chastity, she means chastity.   She portrays Abdrahemen's lust first as a weakness: the Cordobans are the ones that start the tragedy in motion, because *Corruptum viciis cognoscebant Sodomitis* ("they knew that [he] was corrupted by sodomitic vices," 205), and they intend to use Pelagius's adolescent beauty to tempt him. She next portrays the caliph's homosexuality as grotesque: the boy reacts *Magno ridiculo* ("with great ridicule," 241) to the caliph's *Callida...ludicra* ("ludicrous heat," 271).   She has Pelagius intimate that Abdrahemen's homosexuality is pervasive at court, a consequence of his idolatry: *Ergo corde viros licito complectere stultos, / Qui tecum fatuos placantur cespite divos / Sintque tibi socii, servi qui sunt simulacri* ("To uninhibitedly embrace, therefore, the stupid men who with you worship false gods on a turf [altar]; let them be your companions, who are slaves without will").   Finally, she has the fumbling Abdrahemen's dialogue sounding deranged, veering from the desperation of *O lascive puer*, above, to the ghoulish threats of

---

[37] Berschin 170, 171.

Et quod maerentes orbabis forte parentes? / Nostri blasphemos urget cultus cruciandos / subdere mox morti ferro iugulosque forari, ("And why would you, perhaps, bereave your grieving parents? Our rites require that blasphemers be crucified, and undergo death with iron piercing their throats," 266-8), to the cagey offer of the status of consort: *Te quia corde colo necnon venerarier opto / Tanto prae cunctis aulę splendore ministris, / Alter ut in regno sis me prestante superbo* ("Because I [will] cherish you in my heart and choose [you] for favor, to be more splendid than all the ministers in the palace, my second [in command] in the kingdom, me being first," 265-7). O mighty Caesar, dost thou lie so low?

History, however, presents us with a very different mental picture of Moorish Cordoba than does Hrotsvit. In *Pelagius* the young, innocent Christian is brought before the mad caliph; the historical Abd ar-Rahman III, his diplomatic maneuvers having failed, sends a courteous invitation to a shrewd old monk. Hrotsvit's Cordobans get the boy Pelagius prettied up to catch a pederast's eye; in fact, the German ambassador declines a cash stipend from the court to buy presentable clothes.

'Regia,' inquens 'dona non spernor, vestes vero alias praeterquam quibus monacho uti licet, nec pallia prorsus nec eas qui alicuius coloris sunt nisi nigro tantum tinctas aliquatenus induam.' Hoc regi relato: 'Hoc', inquit, 'responso eius constantem animum recognosco. Sacco quoque indutus si veniat, libentissime eum videbo, et amplius mihi placebit.[38]

---

[38] Smith 70.

("I do not disdain the king's gifts, but it is not permitted for a monk to wear clothing other than his usual [garment], nor may I wear clothing dyed any color than black."   When this was told to the king, he said, "By this answer I see the firmness of his mind.   I'll see him gladly, even if he comes wearing a sack.")

Hrotsvit presents us with the image of the young man being showered with unwelcome kisses; in fact, when the ambassador appeared before the caliph, there was kissing of a different sort.

Ut igitur Iohannes coram advenit, manum interne osculandum protenit.   Osculo enim nulli vel suorum vel extraneorum admisso, minoribus quibusque ac mediocribus numquam foris, summis et quos praestantiori excipit pompa, palmam mediam aperit osculandam.[39]

("Then as John [the ambassador] came into his presence, [the caliph] quietly extended his hand to be kissed.   No one, not inside his circle or out, was allowed to kiss his hand, never those of low or middle rank, but of the highest and those of exceptional standing; he opened his palm halfway to be kissed.")

The caliph apologized for the ordeal John had endured: it was nothing personal, as we might say today.   The ambassador, who had intended to verbally unload (the Latin has *evomere*, "spew out") his pent-up resentment at the very tough treatment he had undergone, instead felt suddenly calm, and the two men

---

[39] Smith 72.

conversed on a variety of subjects, and agreed to meet two more times to get to know each other better.   Truth is sometimes stranger than fiction.

An Interpolation:

Retouching an Edward Taylor Touch

Edward Taylor was quasi-anonymous in the same way in the same way that Hrotsvit was: he lived in uneventful times, and lived an uneventful life. He was born in England in 1642, well after the dreadful upheavals of the 30's of that century, and died in Massachusetts in 1729, well before the dreadful French and Indian War. He was known in his day as a pastor, but since the 30's of the twentieth century he has become known for a body of remarkable poetry, devotional in tone and written evidently for his own satisfaction, since the frequency of technical rough spots are evidence of a lack of the sort of polish expended on works intended for publication; the sleekness of Anne Bradstreet's poems, for example, is absent.

Characteristics of Taylor's verse are metric regularity, strong rhymes and forceful imagery. These qualities are not invariable: a line may be short a foot here, a metaphor may be a little stilted there, and, above all, rhymes may become half-rhymes or even no rhymes in the interest of sense. The reader finds attractive variations of tone: there are the learnèd references and turns of phrase that one would expect from a Harvard man conversant with Latin, Greek and Hebrew, but they alternate with charming colloquial passages like the first three lines of *Christ's Reply* (to another poem called *The Soul's Groan to Christ for Succors*):

> Peace, Peace, my Honey, do not Cry,
> My little darling, wipe thine eye,
> Oh Cheer, Cheer up, come see.

Baby simple!   The overall impression is that the poet has much to say, but is not overly self-conscious about how he says it; nor could he have been overly obsessive about occasional loose ends in poetic technique.   A case in point is *A Fig for Thee, Oh! Death.*   It is fifty-six lines long, in iambic pentameter, heroic couplets.   Yet no fewer than six couplets are false rhymes (ll.5,6; 15,16; 23,24; 29,30; 36,37; 47,48).

This should warn the reader not to take Taylor's tidiness as a given: when it occurs, it may be simply a set-up for a jolt. The apparent polish of the *Prologue* to *Preparatory Meditations* is a case in point.   At first it rolls along with Bradstreet-like smoothness: five six-line stanzas, iambic pentameter, ABABCC, strong rhymes.   The poem has a strong, tight, vivid palette as well: the repetition of the phrase "Crumb of Dust," the "list" in stanza two (quill-sharpen-dip-leaves-blot), and colorful compounds ("blot and blur," "jag and jar," "write aright").   The jolt comes in the very last line of the poem, which is a tetrameter, that is, a foot short, which makes the poem end with an attractive syncopated "kick."

A poem in which Taylor's raggedness matches his subject is the aforementioned *A Fig for Thee, Oh! Death,* a poem that is even more powerful than Donne's famous "Death, be not proud."   Why is it not better known?   Here Taylor has been the victim of his editors: the Norton editor defines *fig* as something "valueless, small and contemptible," and this undercuts a very bold Taylor touch, giving this impassioned poem a timid title and a timid ending.   An excursion into the *Oxford English Dictionary* makes it clear that, although "valueless" was within the word's semantic range in Taylor's era (usually it was "a fig's end," though), if it does not literally refer to a fruit, the word almost always refers to an obscene gesture, the thumb between the index and middle finger.   It had, and in much of the Old World still has, all the offensiveness and crudity of The Finger.   A fig for the Norton editor, I say, for vitiating Taylor in this way.   Brought up to date, the title would be *The Finger, Oh! Death, for Thee,* which would match the poem's vehemence; properly understood, the reader feels the fire, the defiance of Taylor's final couplet:

> Although thy terrors rise to th'highest degree,
> I still am where I was.   A Fig for thee.

Anglo-Saxon Anonymity:

Phoenix and *Christ and Satan*

At first glance, nothing seems out of the ordinary about the Old English poem *Phoenix* (*Phx*). It is neither especially long nor especially short (677 lines); its rhythm is the usual stress-stress, caesura, stress-stress; its "music" is, as usual, alliterative; its genre, which I will describe in due course, is not the most common one in Old English poetry, but, as we shall see, is shared by other poems besides *Phx*. The reader is barely into the poem, however, when he is brought up short by the first of a series of anomalies. Lines 15-16 are vigorous, to be sure; "Not blast of frost, not blaze of fire, / Not downpour of hail, not fall of hoarfrost." It is the sound of the words, however, that is arresting.

ne forstes fnæst	*ne fyres blæst*
not frost's blast	not fire's blaze
ne hægles hryre	*ne hrimes dryre*
not hail's downpour	not hoarfrost's fall

Rhyme!   In Anglo-Saxon poetry this is simply not supposed to happen.   Lines 54-55 show that this is not an accident.

> *ne synn ne sacu*   *ne sarwrœcu*
> not sin   not strife   not   misery
> *ne wœdle gewin*   *ne welan onsyn*
> not povery struggle   not riches   lack
> ("Not sin, not strife, not misery, / Not struggle of poverty, not lack of wealth.")

Nor is the "blame" for this very un-Old English anomaly to be traced to the Latin poem that evidently served as the model for *Phx,* as can be seen in the lines in it that correspond to the first of the rhyming passages above (I can find no passage in the Latin original that is close to the second.)

> *Non ibi tempestas nec vis furit horrida venti*   21.
> *Nec gelido terram rore pruina tegit.*
> ("There no storm rages, nor bristling force of the wind, nor does the hoarfrost touch the earth with frozen dew.")

The unique charms of *Phx* have to do less with technical details such as these than with intangibles like its tone: instead of the high drama of action pieces like *Exodus* or the psychological profundity of *Beowulf (Bwf),* the mood of *Phx* is as close as Anglo-Saxon epic ever comes to being sunny; its message of hope and regeneration is serene, understated.   Nor is this cheeriness merely attributable to the author's native woodnotes wild, to a spontaneous outpouring of an amiable personality; I know of no other poem in the Anglo-Saxon corpus that is so self-consciously "arty," either in the sense of "art" proper, or in the sense of "the art of concealing the art."   It is also arty in the sense of being part of a literary continuum: strictly speaking, two continua, a Latin one and an Old English one, and it is a commentary on other literary works, as well as being inspired by other literary works.

It is this last sense that I wish to make my starting point. Originality is a prime parameter in assessing any literary work, and *Phx* does not exist in a vacuum. A discussion of the characteristics of its Latin antecedent is in order, as is a discussion of the Old English genre it represents.

We begin with the Latin. The first 380 lines of *Phx* are an exuberant reworking of *Carmen de ave phoenice* ("The Song of the Phoenix-bird," to be referred to in this chapter as *Carmen,* following Blake, whose edition of both poems is the basis of the present discussion). *Carmen* is written in what are called elegiac couplets, that is, a line of dactylic hexameter followed by a "pentameter" (actually two half-lines of two-and-a-half feet each). Any passage in the poem could be used to illustrate this meter, since the rhythm of the poem is strict throughout; I choose lines 11-14, which concern the bird's idyllic habitat. A line-by-line translation is: "When the heavens blazed with Phaeton's fires, / that place was untouched by the flames, / and when the Flood submerged the world, / it towered over the waters of Deucalion." Using musical notation the meter could be expressed as follows:

♩　　♪ ♪/ ♩　♩/♩ ♩ / ♩　　♪ ♪/ ♩ ♪ ♪　♩ ♩ //
Cum Pha-e- thon-te -is fla- gras-set ab ig-ni-bus a-xis

♩ ♪♪/ ♩　♩ / ♩ // ♩　♪♪/♩ ♪ ♪/♩ //
Il-le lo- cus flam-mis / in-vi-o-la-tus e-rat,

♩　♩　/　♩♪　♪/♩　　♩/♩　♩/♩　♪　♪/♩　♩//
Et cum di-lu-vi-um mer-sis-set fluc-ti-bus or-bem,

♩　　♪♪/♩　♩/♩　//　♩　♪　♪/♩　♪♪/♩//
Deu-ca-li-　o-ne-　as　//　ex-su-pe -ra-vit a-quas.

The reader put off by musical notation may prefer a couplet[1] that, although lacking in *gravitas,* is the best illustration of the rhythm I have ever seen.   The hexameter:

> *Down in a deep dark dell sat an old sow chewin' a beanstalk.*

and the pentameter:

> *Out of her mouth came forth, grunts of a greedy delight.*

The *Carmen* is usually attributed to the fourth-century poet Lactantius, a pagan who converted to Christianity.[2]   There has been some question as to whether the poem dates to the years before his conversion or after.   The reader will recall, however, that in the passage just cited, it is not Noah's flood, but Deucalion's, and it is Phaeton's interruption of the sun's course, not Joshua's.   This is in no way atypical of the rest of the poem: I also find allusions to Aurora, Mercury (indirectly), Venus (twice), and no fewer than five to Phoebus.   I find no Christian

---

[1]   Smith 92.
[2]   Bradley 284.

references. This would seem to settle the matter, but Blake, considering the same facts, draws a conclusion that requires commentary: "In the *Carmen,* however, there are references only to heathen gods and goddesses, and these are included *for rhetorical purposes alone* [italics mine].   There is no suggestion in the *Carmen* that there is one deity who guides and governs all."[3]   I am at a loss as to how Blake can read Lactantius' mind after all these years as to that poet's rhetorical purposes; I take the pagan references at face value: pagan means not Christian.   In the same vein, I do not regard Lactantius' absence of opinion as to the existence of God Almighty as a metaphor for something else; I interpret it simply as a lack of opinion.   Let us stay close to the ground.   If internal evidence means anything, then *Carmen* is a pagan production.

Lactantius' fluency with heathen images, however, is not the only parameter that can give us insight as to his mind when he wrote the *Carmen.*   Besides his religious background, there is much that we can infer about his literary background.

The *Carmen* abounds in Virgilian echoes.   In line 119 there is *Unguine balsameo myrraque et ture Sabaeo* ("with balsamic unguent and myrrh and Sabaean frankincense"), which recalls *Georgics* 1.57 *molles sua tura Sabaei?* ("[how] the soft Sabaeans [send their] frankincense?"), and , less exactly, two other passages (*Georgics* 2.117 and *Aeneid* 1.416-7).   A more definite Virgilian echo is in the *Carmen*'s line 73: *Tum ventos claudit pendentibus Aeolus antris,* ("Then Aeolus closes the

---

[3]   Blake 27.

winds in cliffside caves,"), which would seem to be a telescoped version of *Aeneid* 1.53-5.

> *hic vasto rex Aeolus antro*
> *luctantis ventos tempestatesque sonoras*
> *imperio premit ac vinclis et carcere frenat.*

("Here in a vast cave / Aeolus keeps the battling winds and roaring storms down, and holds them in check, chained and imprisoned.")

If Lactantius knew his Virgil, he must have known his Ovid; rather than literary antecedents, however, Ovid will be our transition to the iconography of the phoenix. Blake provides a detailed account of the evolution of the legend from very remote antiquity, from pharaonic Egypt, as a matter of fact, but it is an open question as to how much of this development Lactantius knew. It seems safer to begin in the middle of Blake's discussion. "In general, classical authors have little to say about the immolation or rebirth of the phoenix, which in Christian and late pagan authors became the kernel of the myth."[4] Lactantius, in fact, does spend much of his time describing the bird's Eden-like habitat. Blake notes a passage in Martial where Rome's "rebirth" under the emperors is compared to the phoenix,[5] but the "center of gravity" for accounts that emphasize the motif of the phoenix's resurrection (as opposed to its habitat and its association with spices) would be toward the middle of the present era.

---

[4] Blake 10.
[5] Blake 10.

A final note about the Latin poem: it is 170 lines long. Since the Old English one is 677 lines, as has been stated, this immediately raises the question of fidelity: is the Anglo-Saxon version's greater length warranted, or is it mere garrulousness? We will deal with this specific question in time, after general comments on passages in the Old English corpus that relate to our topic.

If, as a thought experiment, we were to consider *Phx* only in the context of the other Old English poems that have come down to us, as if its extra-insular antecedents did not exist, we would have to conclude that its "art" in the first sense is completely English, both as to technique (rhythm, alliteration and the poet's "palette" of images) and as to the intangibles like pace and tone.   When we extend our thought experiment, comparing Phoenix with its continental antecedents, we fine "art" in the second sense, of craftsmanship, a painstaking transmutation of foreign, even recalcitrant material.

On the English side, we must acknowledge at the outset that apples-to-apples comparison is difficult, because there are not many apples.   I hope that the reader will allow me some leeway in my terminology here: I will refer to *Phx* as a didactic reverie, a term which I use in preference to the commonly-used "dream vision," since the "vision" is what is important; the sleeping is incidental.   I concede that the *Phx* is poet says that he has *heard* of the phoenix, not that he has dreamed of it, but I argue that the didacticism of the poem calls for it to be classified with other works that we will consider.   (A new term will be needed, in any case, to match the new reality that will exist when the study of Anglo-Saxon prose, especially the homiletic literature, becomes as advanced as the study of Anglo-Saxon poetry; I predict a synthesis of the two that will change the way that we look that we look at Old English literature.)   Whether we call it didactic reverie or dream vision, however, we must admit at the outset that in this genre Anglo-Saxon literature is thin.   The sublime *Dream of the Rood* is one example, or three if we take the short inscriptions on the Ruthwell Cross and the Brussells Cross as a sort of mini-family, allowing for the uncertainty of their affiliations.   There are dreams in a companion-piece in the Junius book, the epic *Daniel,* but it could be argued that they are the result, not of the poet's literary intentions, but of the poet's fidelity to the Vulgate original.

This last sentence requires clarification: the *Daniel* poet is faithful the Vulgate version insofar as he includes the two dreams, but his fidelity in the case of the first dream extends no further.   Quite the contrary: the *Daniel* version is a cadenza so exuberant, so arbitrary, that it would be worth the reader's attention even in isolation.   In the context of the present discussion, however, it is an antidote to the criticism that *Phx* is wordy and repetitious, that it falls short of the terseness of the Latin original.[6]   I trust that the reader will indulge a digression in which I spell this out: the present discussion is, after all, only a partial treatment of this very tangled question, and a clearly-understood benchmark will be of use as we proceed.

We may take it that the account of Nebuchadnezzar's dreams in the Vulgate was the *Daniel* poet's point of departure. Let us examine the first verse of the second chapter.

---

[6]   Blake 5.

In anno secundo regni Nabuchodonosor, vidit Nobuchodonosor somnium, et conterritus est spiritus eius, et somnium eius fugit ab eo.

("In the second year of the reign of Nebuchadnezzar, Nebuchadnezzar saw a dream, and his spirit was terrified, and his sleep fled from him.")

This simple, neat statement becomes a farrago of no fewer than sixteen lines in the *Daniel* poet's reworking.

Þa wæs breme   Babilone weard,
then was glorious   Babylon's keeper
mære and modig   ofer middangeard, 105.
glorious and proud   over   earth

(Another rhyme, I admit, but I take it as nothing more than an unimportant coincidence.)

egesful ylda   bearnum. No   he ae fremede,
dreadful of-men to-the children not-at-all he law   did
ac in oferhygde   æghwæs   lifde.
but in   pride   in-every-way lived
Þa þam   folctogan on frumslæpe
then to-that   leader   in   first-sleep
siððan to reste gehwearf rice þeoden, 110.
after   to rest   went   mighty lord
com on   sefan hwurfan swefnes woma,
came into   mind   go   of-dreamnoise
hu woruld wære   wundrum geteod,
how world would-be   wonderfully made

ungelic yldum oð edsceafte.

unlike   for-men until re-creation

Wearð him on slæpe soð   gecyðed,

came to-him   in   sleep truth made-known

þætte rices gehwæs reðe sceolde gelimpan, 115.

of-that realm   each   cruelly should   happen

eorðan dreamas, ende wurðan.

of-earth's joy   end   became

Þa onwoc wulfheort,   se   ær   wingal swæf,

then woke   wolf-heart,   who earlier   drunken sleep

Babilone weard. Næshimbliðe   hige,

Babylon's   keeper was-not to-him glad mind

ac him   sorh   astah, swefnes woma.

but to-him anxiety arose of-dream noise

*No   he gemunde   þæt   him   meted wæs.*120.

not-at-all he remembered   what to-him dreamed was

("Then was the lord of Babylon vainglorious, renowned
and proud throughout the world, frightening to the children
of men.   He obeyed no law, and lived arrogantly in every
way.   Soon after this leader had gone to sleep, after the
mighty lord had gone to rest, there came into his mind the
sound of a dream, how the world would be changed,
different from the Creation.   In sleep the truth was
revealed to him that there would occur a cruel end to the
kingdom and the joys of earth.   Then the wolf-heart awoke,
he who had earlier passed out from drinking.   His mind
was not glad, and anxiety arose in him, the sound of a
dream.   He did not remember at all what he had
dreamed.")

Since the Biblical Nebuchadnezzar is not exactly Prince Charming, the *Daniel* poet's exuberant extra-Biblical editorializing at his expense here may seem like a sort of gilding the lily in reverse. To be fair, his versification of the second dream is much more workmanlike, being true to the Vulgate account both in length and content, as can be seen from the following sample–passage. First, the Vulgate Daniel, 4:7-8.

> *Videbam, et ecce arbor in medio terrae, et altitudo eius nimia. Magna arbor, et fortis, et proceritas eius contingens caelum; aspectus illius erat usque ad terminus universae terrae. Folia eius pulcherrima, et fructus eius nimius, et esca universorum in ea.*
>
> ("I saw, and behold, a tree in the middle of the earth, and its height was enormous. A great tree, and strong, and its height touching heaven; it could be seen all the way to the ends of the earth. Its leaves were very beautiful, and it was laden with fruit, and the food of all was in it.")

Again, simple and neat. The *Daniel* poet this time continues in the same vein. Nebuchadnezzar, we note, sounds nothing like the earlier bibulous wolf-heart.

*Þa   him   wearð on slæpe swefen ætywed.*495.
then to-him occurred in sleep dream shown
Nobochodonossor; him   þæt neh gewearð.
Nebuchadnezzar   to-him that near happen
Þuhte   him Þæt on foldan fægres stode
seemed to-him that on earth   fair   stood

wudubeam wlitig, se wæs wyrtum   fæst,
tree   beautiful it was as-for-roots firm
beorht on blædum.   Næs he bearwe gelic,
bright   as-for-leaves was-not it grove   like
ac he hlifode to heofontunglum, 500.
but it towered to   heaven's stars
swilce he oferfæðmde foldan sceatas,
like wise it   covered   of-earth regions
ealne middangeard, oð merestreamas,
   all   earth   until   waves
twigum   and   telgum.
with-twigs   and   with-branches
("Then in his sleep a dream was revealed to Nebuchadnezzar
that hit close to home.   It seemed to him that there was a
beautiful tree, bright-leaved and firmly rooted in the earth.
It was not like a tree in a grove, but towered to the stars of
heaven, extended over the four corners of the earth, as far
as the ocean.")

In the epic *Elene* there is a vision that includes a tree that is
not called for in the original.

Geseah he   frætwum   beorht
Saw   he with-ornaments bright
wliti   wuldres   treo ofer wolcna hrof.
beautiful of-glory tree   over   cloud roof
gold   egeglenged, (gimmas lixtan);90.
with-gold adorned   gems   shone
wæs   se blaca beam bocstafum awriten,
there-was the shining tree   with-letters inscribed

beorhte ond leohte: "Mid þys beacne ðu
bright   and   clear   with this   sign   you
on þam frecnan   fære   feond oferswiðesð,
on this   terrible expedition enemy you-overcome
geltetest lað   werod."
With stand   hateful host

("He saw, bright with adornments, a beautiful tree of glory over the cloud-roof, adorned with gold, gems shone, there was the shining tree, inscribed with letters, bright and light: 'With this sign you will overcome the enemy on this terrible expedition; you will withstand the hateful host.'")

The opening verses will remind the reader of the most famous example of this genre.

Þuhte me þæt ic gesawe syllicre treow
thought   I   that I   saw   marvelous tree
on lyft lædan   leohte   bewunden, 5.
on   air   bear   with-light   enveloped
beama beorhtost. Eall þæt beacen wæs
    tree   brightest   all   that vision   was
boegten mid golde: gimmas stodon
covered   with gold   gems   stood
fægre   æt foldan sceatum, swylce þær fife wæron
beautiful   at earth's   surface   which there five   were
uppe on þæm eaxlgespanne
    up   on   the   crossbeam

("I thought that I saw a marvelous tree raised on high, enveloped in light, brightest of trees. All the image was covered with gold. Beautiful on earth, gems were set, five of them, up on the crossbeam.")

This of course, from *The Dream of the Rood.* This leads us back to *Phx,* where the bird perches in yet another gratuitous tree.

Þær he heanne beam on holtwuda
there he high tree in grove
wunað ond weardað wyrtym fæstne
dwell and inhabit as-to-roots secure
under heofumhrofe, þone hatað men
under roof-of-heaven which call men
fenix on foldan of þæs fugles noman.
"phoenix" on earth after this bird's name
Hafað þam treowe forgiefen tirmeahtig Cyning,175.
has to-it tree bestowed almighty King
Meotud moncynnes, mine gefræge,
Lord of-mankind my report
þæt se ana is ealra beama
that it unique is of-all trees
on eorðwege uplændra
on earth tall
beorhtast geblowen.
brightest blossoming

("There [the Phoenix] lives in a tall tree in a grove, firmly rooted under heaven; men on earth call it 'phoenix,' after the bird. The almighty King, Lord of mankind, so I have heard, bestowed the tree to it, unique among all trees for being tall and brightest-blooming.")

All these trees must not make us lose sight of the forest.   We have discussed a variety of examples of a literary theme without the necessity of invoking any authorial materials at all.   How important, then, is authorship?   I concede that *Elene* is not strictly anonymous, since it includes the runic signature of Cynewulf, but this Cynewulf is otherwise only a name to us.   If "Cynewulf" should turn out to be a pseudonym, then we are left with nothing more than a tag, as unhelpful as the tags "*Phx* poet" or "*Daniel* poet."

The most significant obstacle to understanding the Anglo-Saxon epic *Christ and Satan* is its title.   *Christ and Satan*, after all, suggests a confrontation between Jesus and the Devil, but the reader who expects this finds himself confronted instead with a series of lamentations of Satan in hell, an account of the fall of the apostate angels, and homilies that urge the poem's audience to avoid the sin of pride and fix their thoughts on heaven.   It is not until the end of the poem, line 667 of a total of 733 lines, that a face-off takes place, or rather the beginning of a face-off: the author begins a poetic version of the Temptation of Christ, but the account is incomplete, and the poem ends — or rather, breaks off — with Satan back in hell (lines 711-733).   At the first reading, the reader is left with an impression of disorderliness.   This impression, as I say, comes from false expectations raised by the title of the work; nevertheless, in this study I will refer to the poem as *Christ and Satan* (*CaS*), simply because that is the way that the poem has been referred to for several hundred years now, in the critical continuum.   The reader would do well to remember, however, that the epic, in the form that it has come down to us, has no title. In order to avoid preconceptions and see the poem as it is, then, he must from time to time *remember to forget* the title that has been tacked on.   Seen on its own terms, *CaS* is a fine work, not only when it is read to give context to other Old English poetry, but for its own literary worth.   True, there are times when its author gets tangled in distracting stylistic mannerisms, but more often he writes with great power.

Before concentrating on the poem itself, a preliminary note is in order concerning its subject: rebel angels and a soliloquizing Satan must remind the English–speaking reader of Milton's *Paradise Lost*.   Clubb, in fact, whose fine edition of *CaS* is the basis for the present study, intersperses his commentary and notes[7] with quotations from Milton, as if *Paradise Lost* were what the *CaS* poet were trying for, and not attaining.   Quite the contrary: *CaS* is clearly superior to *Paradise Lost*.   Milton's epic is built on sand, the false idea that poetry is inherently superior to prose, or, stated more fully, that the perfectly good prose narrative in the Bible is inherently inferior to bombastic poetry.   The *CaS* poet proceeds from the same false assumption, true, but on a humbler, more respectful scale, and so his aesthetic transgression is nothing like the breathtaking narcissism of Milton's rant.

Now, to the poem: *CaS* is an Anglo-Saxon poem of 733 lines of unknown authorship and date.   There appear to be two gaps in the manuscript, but the poem is nevertheless coherent, and is considered to be the work of one author by the scholarly consensus.[8]   From a literary standpoint, *CaS* is noteworthy for its author's evident familiarity with other Old English epics, especially *Guthlac A*:   many turns of phrase are so similar that

---

[7] Clubb *passim*.
[8] Clubb xlii.

the author of one poem seems to have been writing with the word-hoard of the other in mind, although it is not clear who is borrowing from whom. *Elene, Exodus, Daniel* and *Phx* are other epics with less frequent points of contact.

(As for *Bwf*, a prefatory note is order: I take *Bwf* to be a late work whose author made use of the word-hoards of many, if not all of these earlier works for purposes of poetic background, for the techniques involved in setting a tone of seriousness and dignity appropriate to an epic. The similarities between the earlier works are evident because their topics are the same [homiletic commentaries on Biblical narratives, with *Phx* being a separate sub-genre, as noted above], and because their authors' talents are on the same level [masters of the genre, true, but not world-class artists]. The *Bwf* poet, on the other hand, was a world-class artist, and chose a topic [legends of the Danelaw] that was more romantic (in the modern sense of the word) and that lent itself to a grander scope and a more theatrical unfolding than the boxed-in, self-contained didacticism that the earlier works would permit. These two factors group *Elene, Phx, Guthlac A, Daniel* and *Exodus* together, and leave *Bwf* in a class by itself.)

Other characteristics of the *CaS* poet are his boldness with transitions, his love of echo, and his reliance on trenchant one-liners. Considering these traits in reverse order, the poet's habit of putting all his eggs in one basket is sometimes powerful, as in line 97b, which caps a comparison of vanished heavenly bliss with present hellish torment:

> *Ic   eom   fah   wið   God.*
> I   am   foe against God
> ("I am God's enemy.")

On the other hand, there are times when the *CaS* poet falls flat. Fatally for the poem, its last half-line is just such a dud: after constructing a vivid panorama that leads the reader from before the creation of man to the present, and all the way through heaven and hell, and after a final grim look at Satan in hell, the poet caps his set-up by having the fiends who Satan has led to damnation begin

> *reordian and cweðan*   *732b.*
>   to talk   and   say

At 162b, as we shall see, the *CaS* poet presents a much more forceful and believable description of speech under duress than this colorless "to talk and say."

> *"La! þus beo   nu   on yfele ..." 733a.*
>   hey thus be-you henceforth in   evil
> ("Ha! so be you henceforth accursed;")

And then the stinger:

> *"...noldæs   ær   teala."*
>   you-did-not-wish   formerly   aright

As for the dreadful blandness of that last half-line, Charles W. Kennedy's translation[9] captures it perfectly: "Thou didst not wish for good." Apparently the *CaS* poet calculated that "Thou didst not wish for good" was the way to end his poem

---

9   Kennedy 15.

with a bang; he misjudged. *Parturiunt montes, nascitur ridiculus mus* ("the mountains are in labor, and a ridiculous mouse is born"), as Horace said.   I stress that this insipid ending would not be a fault if *CaS* were an insipid poem.   *CaS* is a very good poem, but sometimes, as Horace also said, good Homer nods.

The second characteristic of the *CaS* poet that I have mentioned is his love of echo, which he also uses with varying degrees of success.   By "echo" I do not mean alliterative echo, which is a constant in OE verse.   I mean exact or nearly exact repetitions (allowing for scribal orthographic idiosyncrasies) of words or phrases.   This is to be seen on the very first page of *CaS*:   line 4 has *Seolfa he gesette*   ("he himself created"), which is echoed in line 13 as *seolua he gesette*, to all intents and purposes nothing more than an orthographic variant (*u* for *f*) of the same.   "Through his" is not an evocative phrase, but the poet gives us three of them, all on the first page, and all on the second half-line.

> *ðurh   his wundra miht* 6b.
> through his wonder's might
> *þurh   his soðan miht 13b.*
> through his   true   might
> *þurh   his wuldres Gast 14b.*
> through his   glory's   spirit

Echo can be a very effective technique in OE verse, but not if it seems mechanical.

At times, however, the *CaS* poet uses the echo technique to achieve an almost operatic power, as in one of the outbursts of Satan in hell (162b-168).

> *Word spearcum   fleah*
> Speech   like-sparks   flew [out]
> *attre   gelicost,   þonne   he   ut   þorhdraf:*
> poison   like   which   he   out   spat

"His words flew out like sparks; he spat them out like venom" is much superior to the "talk and say" noted earlier.

> *Eala   Drihtenes   þrym!   eala   duguða   Helm!*
> oh   Lord's   glory   oh   host's   protector
> *eala   Meotodes   miht!   eala   middaneard!   165.*
> oh   creator's   might   oh   earth
> *eala   dæg   leohta!   eala   dream   Godes!*
> oh   day   light   oh   joy   of God
> *eala   engla   þreat!   eala   upheofen!*
> oh   angels'   throng   oh   highest heaven
> *eala   þæt ic eam ealles   leas   ecan   dreames*
> oh   that I   am   of-all   destitute   of-eternal   [of-] joy

This passage is simply wonderful: the exclamation *eala* is certainly an honest word to repeat, and the way the e:a vowels carry over to line 168, with *eam*, *ealles*, *leas* and *dreames* creates an echo in a musical sense, in the acoustic sense of a dying reverberation that suggests the vastness of the halls of hell.

This splendid passage notwithstanding, with the *CaS* poet echo is more often than not a mere mannerism.   There is a fine passage in which Christ commands Satan to take the measure of hell, literally.

> *Wite   þu   eac,   awyrgda,   hu   wid and sid*

know thou also   accursed   how wide and broad
hel heorodreorig, and mid hondum amet: *700.*
hell   mournful   and with   hands measure
("Learn, accursed one, how wide and broad woeful
hell is; measure it with your hands!")

In response, just as his poem should be building to a final climax,
the CaS poet lapses into a repetition of, of all words, *hwilum*
("sometimes, then"), which is one of the least evocative words
imaginable, and places the series in one of the most exposed
positions imaginable, on the second half-line (emphases mine).

<u>*Hwilum*</u> *mid folmum mæt*
         then   with hands measured
*wean and   witu.   *<u>*Hwilum*</u>* se wonna   leg   715.*
woe and torments   then the dark   flame
læhte   wið   þes laþan. <u>*Hwilum*</u>* he licgan geseah,*
flared-up toward the fiend   then he to-lie   saw
hæftas in hylle. <u>*Hwilum*</u>* ream astag,*
captives in hell   then   clamor arose
ðonne he on þone atolan eagum gesawun.
when they on that monster with-eyes gazed
("<u>Then</u> with his hands [Satan] measured off [the place of]
woe and torments. <u>Then</u> the dark flame surged against
the fiend. <u>Then</u> he saw [his fellow] captives in hell lyng
there. <u>Then</u> a howl uprose, when they laid eyes on that
monster.")

The last of the three style traits I mentioned above, the *CaS*
poet's boldness with transitions, is his forte. Throughout the

work scene follows scene with effective use of unexpected content. The opening of *CaS* concerns the Creation, and its tone of grandeur sets up a forceful, abrupt change of direction on the half-line of line 21 (emphasis mine).

> *Adam ærest, and þæt æðele cyn,*   *20.*
> Adam   first   and that   noble species
> *engla ordfruman, þæt   þe   eft   forwarð.*
> angels'   princes   that   which   afterward was-destroyed

The reader is thus unexpectedly propelled into the matter of the fall of the apostate angels.   The *CaS* poet consistently uses the element of surprise to move the drama forward.

After an eleven-line account of the fall of the angels, the *CaS* poet has Satan take center stage (34) with a contrast of hell and heaven.   The fallen angels denounce him in chorus (53), after which there is a homily on pride from the poet (65).   The frequent changes of viewpoint are noteworthy, and add an extra parameter to the narrative. Satan's second speech (81) is a reprise of the first, but more anguished: it is in the first person, specific details of his misery are recounted, and we learn that the Devil may fly forth from hell (112) from time to time.   His third speech (130) emphasizes the torments of hell, and we learn that Satan's gigantic size makes the halls of hell seem cramped.   The tempo and intensity of his outcries increase, impelled not so much by his vocabulary as by his swings from this grievance to that: now he laments the loss of his heavenly home, now he regrets his war against God, now he rages against the tortures he suffers.   The effect is one of seething instability.

Then, without any transition, comes a sudden calm, a homiletic aside to the reader:

> *Forþan sceal   gehycgan hæleða æghwylc*
>   hence should   take-heed   man   each
> *þæt he ne abelige Bearn Waldendes;*   195.
>   that he not offend   son   of-sovereign

("Therefore let every man take heed that he not offend the Son of God.")

The tone of mild reproof modulates from an exhortation to avoid the damnation of the apostates to an invitation to delight.

> *Neoman us to wynne weoroda Drihten,*   198.
>   choose we for delight of-hosts   lord
> *uppe ecne gefean, engla   Waldend*
>   above eternal joy   angels'   ruler

and, modulating in turn into language reminiscent of *Phx,* to the assurance that heaven is

> *fægere land, þonne þeos folde seo*   213.
>   a fairer land   than   this earth could- be

The narrator uses a one-line transition to bring us back to hell, but this time to a mood of regret: the devils acknowledge their guilt (230) and recall their idyllic former state.   The *CaS* poet has an especially subtle transition from the demons to the Devil (248), indicated only by the transition from "we" to "I." The Devil reprises his activities fomenting rebellion, then transitions directly to the apostates' present state, alternating between prostrate misery in hell and flying over the earth to spread misery there; we are told that even when flying around, however, the evil spirits are cocooned in fire, so their punishment never stops.

(The image of a malevolent fiery being flying through the air will remind the reader of the dragon in *Bwf.* In addition to the similarities between the word-hoards of *CaS* and *Guthlac A*, Clubb lists points of contact with *Bwf* as well, and there are quite a number. This should surprise no one. As I have said above, I take *Bwf* to be a late work, in which the *Bwf* poet made use of the existing poetic conventions of Anglo-Saxon verse in vocabulary and style; it may be that he designed his dragon with the literary experience and expectations of his audience in mind as well.)

The *CaS* poet commits a slight inconsistency in line 273: as Satan continues his speech about the fiends flying through the air, he says *Ic her geþolian sceal* ("I must suffer <u>here</u>," emphasis mine), in contrast to their mobility. Let us not read too much into this line. Before and after this speech the *CaS* poet portrays Satan as going to and fro in the earth, and walking up and down in it, as the writer of the book of Job would say, and in the underworld as well. In any case, it will not do to let one word, <u>her</u>, distract us from the whole speech, whose tone is consistently elegiac rather than anguished, again using variety of mood to keep the narrative fresh.

The transition to the homily that follows is achieved by a variation on the I/we mutation observed above. Line 276 has "I;" the following line asks if "we" (evidently including the apostate angels) will ever be reconciled to God; the homily begins with God's anger at "them" (280)   The transition from singular to plural is artful, using the ambiguity of "we" as a pivot. The body of the homily is directed at "us," evidently humans, who are urged to have faith in God, and the description of heaven is the grandest, most vivid one yet.

Then, with one word, the exclamation *eala*, the scene plunges back into hell.   The poet particularizes the image with more specifics.

Nabbað hē tō hyhte   nymþe hāt and cyle,   *335.*
not-have they for hope   except   hot and cold
wean and   witu   and   wyrma   þreat,
  woe   and suffering and   snakes'   swarm
dracan and næddran, and þone dimman ham.
Dragons and   vipers   and that   murky   home

The *CaS* poet follows this persuasive evocation of the horrors of hell with a stylistic surprise, a combination of description and homily (355).   An account of heaven would be more or less expected, since the torments of the damned have just been recounted, but a moralizing exhortation in which the joys of heaven are described is an unexpected device, and prepares the reader for a change of pace, in this case the feeling of a finale, since a narrative of the harrowing of hell begins at 366.

Before moving on, however there are two loose ends to tie up.   We note first a stylistic detail: *nymþe* (335) is another of the *CaS* poet's echoes.   He uses it before (331) and after (350). Since "except" is not an especially powerful word, its repetition is not especially effective.

Then there is a phrase, *fæstlic þreat*, that requires commentary, because as Kennedy translates it, it would seem to revive the <u>her</u> business I have noted on line 273 above, the idea of Satan's being unable to move in hell. The Old English word *fæstlic* is cognate with the modern "fast" (in the sense of "firm"). *Þreat* is a group; we have earlier noticed *wyrma þreat* ("a swarm of snakes"). Here is the passage in full.

þonne wæs heora aldor, þe ðær ærest com
  then was their prince, who there first came
forð on feþan, þæt wæs fæstlic þreat. 325.
  forth in host that was steady company

("Then was their prince, who came there [to hell] before [the others] / preeminent in [that] company. That was a resolute company.")

Kennedy translates these two lines as "And their prince, who came there first of all the host, was fettered fast in fire and flame; that was unending torment."[10] The problem is that Kennedy translates *fæstlic* twice, once ("fettered") in the sense of meaning "unmoving," as in its modern form of "fasten," and once ("unending") in the figurative sense of "constant." This temporal sense is certainly within the word's semantic range: *Exodus* has

               Wræcmon gebad
                exiles awaited
laðne lastweard, se ðe him lange ær
  enemy following that which them long past

---

[10] Kennedy 7.

> *eðelleasum   onnied gescraf,*
> lacking-a-homeland oppression assigned
> *wean witum   fœst,* 140.
> woe torment constant

("The exile [Israelites] awaited the following [Egyptian] foe, which had long since dealt them, without a country as they were, constant woe and torment.")

A greater divergence of opinion involves *þreat*, which I take in its usual sense, of a group, and which Kennedy evidently takes as a form of *geþrēatian* ("torment"). True, *Elene* has *hungre geþreatod* ("tormented with hunger," 695), and *Juliana* has *þreat ormœte* ("excessive torment," 495) a passage especially compelling since both the preceding and the following line include the word *þolian* ("undergo").

I take *fœstlic* in its literal sense, "steady," because I take *þreat* in its literal sense, and consider *fœstlic þreat* to be one of those holdovers from the days when epics were martial. *The Dream of the Rood*'s description of Jesus as *þa geong hœleð* ("the young warrior") as he mounts the Cross has is well known, but it is often spoken of as a bold touch on the part of the author; yet the Anglo-Saxon poets constantly spoke with a military accent. In *CaS*, *hœleð* is used in this way (47), but also for wavering humanity, as we have already noted (194). Military turns of phrase are part of the Old English poetic vocabulary, regardless of the subject being treated. As for *fœstlic*, I cite two familiar passages in *The Battle of Maldon*.

> *ac   hi fœstlice wið   ða fynd weredon   82.*
> and they steadily against   enemy defended

("and stoutly defended themselves against the enemy")
feaht fæstlice, fleam he forhogode   *254.*
fought stoutly   flight he   despised
("he fought stoutly, he scorned flight")

More than for any other reason, I translate *CaS* 325b, *þæt wæs fæstlic þreat*, as "that was [a] resolute company" on the analogy of *Bwf*'s familiar *þæt wæs god cyning* ("that was [a] good king," 11). If this be humdrum, so be it. Let us stick to knowns.

After the sustained optimism of the homily there is another transition, remarkable for its rapidity: the beauty of heaven, the former beauty of Lucifer, the pride of Lucifer, the damnation of Lucifer and his legions, and the commotion in hell at the approaching Harrowing: the righteous are joyful, the unrighteous are terrified (366-382). There is a chorus of lamentation from the fiends (384-399). The Harrowing itself is presented succinctly, as irresistible, overwhelming, decisive. Jesus begins to ascend to heaven with the righteous (400-408a).

Then, just as the ascent is beginning, the *CaS* poet presents us with a double surprise. When we least expect it, we hear a voice that we least expect: Eve, who is about to be left behind, speaks out, and the gigantic event of the Harrowing stops cold at the sound of a mortal woman's voice. Eve's speech is remarkable for its sudden *pianissimo* after the roar of the conflict, but also for its sudden change of pace. The *CaS* poet has been tightening up the narrative's momentum: the transition from the homily noted above comes to sixteen lines; the apostates' chorus is fifteen lines; the Harrowing is eight; Eve's speech is thirty-four lines long, which makes it not only an abrupt, we could say lurching, change from *forte* to *pianissimo*, but also from *agitato* to an unhurried *andante*. So unhurried is the passage that the poet even takes time to insert stage directions: *Ræhte þa mid handum to Heofencyninge* ("she reached out with her hands to the heaven-king," 437).

(Let us briefly turn our mind's eye from the scene the *CaS* poet has depicted and try to imagine a scene a mere thousand years ago, in Anglo-Saxon England, a mead-hall or a monastery refectory where *CaS* is being declaimed. *CaS* is ideal for public performance because its frequent changes of tone and narration are an actor's dream-come-true. "Actor" may not be the right word, since it implies a career; the reader may substitute "declaimer" or some such term, but only if the word implies extroverted delivery, or, less gracefully, hamming it up. Not "reciter" or "reader:" I cannot imagine *CaS* being rendered in a monotonous, nasal sing-song, then or now. Anyone who reads the poem aloud must get caught up in its theatricality, adopting a Satan-voice here and a heaven-voice there. *CaS* is an ideal performance set-piece.)

Eve's appeal is successful. After Christ leads the rescued souls from hell, he refers to her as *þæt æðele wif* ("that noble woman," 473). In the same speech, the Fall of Man is recapitulated; in her speech Eve has described the Fall from her point of view, now Christ describes it from his, and then goes on to describe the Crucifixion. The address is a full forty-two lines long. Beginning with 514 the *CaS* poet recounts the events from the Resurrection to the Ascension, then depicts Christ in heaven as mediator.

(The scene beginning with line 569 should be mentioned before proceeding, since it is a rare misidentification by the otherwise meticulous Clubb: he identifies it as a reference to

Pentecost,[11] but the passage clearly refers to the Last Supper and Judas' betrayal. Taken by itself, putting the Last Supper after the Ascension may seem like nothing more than an artless flashback, but there is also an earlier out-of-sequence episode where, immediately after the matter of Doubting Thomas (543-546), there is a homiletic reflection on the Crucifixion. The reader should note these passages as an introduction to the very serious problems of chronology that must be considered toward the end of *CaS*.)

The *CaS* poet follows his depiction of Jesus in heaven after the Ascension with a compelling description of Judgment Day, and a recapitulation of the pains of hell and the splendors of heaven (600-666).

At 667, without any transition or explanation whatever, the *CaS* poet begins an account of the Temptation of Christ. Unexpected content is one thing, but a break in a narrative's time line is quite another. Yet what the CaS poet has composed is worse than a break; it is a backward ordering of events. We have already noted awkward sequence problems with Ascension-Last Supper and Doubting Thomas-Crucifixion, so this third instance of chronological inconsistency must be addressed. A modern reader may find this mis-ordering too much to accept, and may question whether there is some sort of breakdown in the integrity of the manuscript. This is a fair question. Jumping ahead to line 675, in the middle of the Temptation, after the Devil has brought *brade stanas* ("broad stones," an effective particularization of the image;

---

[11] Clubb 41.

the Vulgate and the Greek simply say "stones") to be made
bread, we find

> *þa him andswarode ece Drihten*   675.
> then him   answered   eternal lord
> *wendest þu, awyrgda, þæt awriten nære*
> suppose   you accursed   that written isn't
> > *nymþe me ænne,*
> > except me alone
> *ac geseted hafast,   sigores Agend,*
> and ordained you-have victory's owner
> *lifigendum liht,   lean   butan ende,*
> for-living   light reward   without end
> *on heofenrice, halige dreamas*
> in heaven-realm holy   joys
> *þa   he   mid hondum genom*
> then he   with hands   took

("Then the eternal Lord answered him, 'Do you suppose,
accursed one, that it is not written...'" "...except me alone,
and you have ordained, Lord of victory, light for the living
in heaven, reward without end..." "The he [Satan] took
[Jesus] in his hands...")

There is clearly some sort of jumble here, but it is not the
only jumble we have encountered. In order to interpret the
poem, the reader must identify each jumble according to type:
if the problem is one of mistransmission, that is, of a medieval
copyist making a mistake in page numbers, the reader can make
a mental adjustment, and the editor can adjust the order on the
page; on the other hand, if these anachronic sequences are

intentional, another mannerism of the poet, then they must be accepted as non-negotiable elements of an artistic package deal. The reader may not like this possibility, since it means that the poem's rambling, careless feeling is the result of the poet's having feet of clay.   I do not like it.   Although I may wish that the *CaS* poet had been tidier, however, I must admit that I am unable to read his mind after all these centuries, and so do not know his intentions.   There is also the question of whether or not the form in which *CaS* has come down to us is complete: the "cast thyself down" part of the Temptation is absent, and for all we know the *CaS* poet did produce a rounded-out conclusion to his narrative that has not survived.   The editors of the poem over the years have been unwilling to rearrange the poem, and so there the matter must rest, as one of the elusive questions in which the study of Old English literature abounds.

A Digression:

Translating *Beowulf*

John McNamara put his finger on the essence of the translator's art in the introduction to his *Beowulf.* "Once again, the value of the translation is to be seen in its loyalty to the original – as a faithful retainer should be to whom the lord has given a great gift."[1]

Loyalty. This is the first time that I have ever heard the word used by a translator. What a fine, one-word antidote for the translator's characteristic vice, the intrusion of his personality between the original and the reader! It is gratifying to note that McNamara's *Beowulf* has been selling well, that readers have responded to his untheatrical craftsmanship and to his loyalty.

By contrast, readers may respond to my *Beowulf* excerpt with a verdict of treason. Setting aside literary concerns, there is the plain fact that it was this same John McNamara who taught me Old English, and who was my first guide into *Beowulf.* A fine student this, to horn in on his teacher's territory! As to those literary concerns, the reader may be equally severe, since my translation ignores parameters that are essential to the original, and intrinsic to all Anglo-Saxon poetry.

---

[1] McNamara xli.

I ask the reader to withhold judgment for the moment.   My translation   is certainly no threat to Dr. McNamara's, and deals with a completely different question: McNamara leads the reader to *Beowulf*; I attempt to lead *Beowulf* to the reader, that is, to take into account the literary preconceptions and expectations of the early twenty-first century.

Many years ago I heard the American poet John Ciardi speak, and the subject of translation came up.   He was midway through his rendering of Dante's *Divine Comedy*, and after observing that "translating *Heaven* is hell," he asked why Heine's *Du bist wie eine Blume* is so flat when translated straight across: You are like a flower.   Flat.   Burns' "My love is like a red, red rose," though, that's poetry; there's nothing flat about that.   Then he suggested that "maybe the best translation for *Du bist wie eine Blume* is 'My love is like a red, red rose.'"

Intangibles aside, poetry is a craft, and a craft is a mosaic of techniques that can be examined separately; when ferrying poetry from one language to another, the success of the translation can be judged parameter by parameter.   A perfect translation of *Beowulf,* it could be argued, would convey the drama of a live performance, either sung or declaimed to music, would have a strongly rhythmic "feel" (the underlying rhythmic pulse that makes the *Beowulf* poet's artful syncopations possible), have prominent Anglo-Saxon style characteristics like alliteration and compound words, avoid both modern anachronisms and phony archaisms, and have a noble tone.

The last of these difficulties is certainly the greatest. Pasternak was only partly right when he said that the language of our times is urban; in fact, the language of our times is urban and snide. Everything is mocked these days (except for the twin sacred cows of sex and drugs), and audiences are quick to giggle. There is a minefield of risqué double entendres that the translator must avoid, but less colorful pitfalls can break the spell as well: the term *bior-sele* does not occur in the passage I have translated, but it is a good example of the hazards of straight-across translation, since "beer-hall" suggests accordions and bright lights; the mood is lost.

The avoidance of modern anachronisms is not hard, since the translator sees the action in his mind's eye. Thus, in line 3125 *æled-lêoman* would not be translated simply as "light," because flashlights and cigarette lighters must be specifically excluded. It is the mind's eye, however, that makes the temptation toward archaism so strong. The mention of a coat of mail, a "ye" here and a "thou" there, and soon one's bad angel is wheedling, trying to justify using words like "prithee" and "eftsoons."

From the "don'ts" we proceed to the "musts." There are traits that are essential to Old English verse that simply do not exist in modern poetry. Alliteration moves the line forward in *Beowulf,* since the ear reaches for the "echo" of the first half of the verse in the second, once the pattern has been set up. Yet today we feel no pull, no incompleteness. In line 3103, *wundur under wealle* stands by itself to the modern reader; by the conventions of Anglo-Saxon verse, however, it is a springboard toward the next section, beginning with *ic êow wîsige,* since the ear will not rest without the half-line being completed. In the same way that alliteration gives momentum from half-line to half-line, the unhurried triple rhythm moves the reader from line to line. The effect must have been natural, seamless to the ancient audience; not to the modern reader.

(I write "triple" advisedly.   If we assume that Beowulf was declaimed to music, then the declaimer must have a place to breathe, and a place to strum his harp.   In a live performance situation, then, the caesura is not just a hiccough, but a meaningful and natural pause.   Thus the meter is not stress, stress (gasp) stress, stress, but rather
strummmm, stress, stress, strummmm, stress, stress,
that is,
harp, sing, sing, harp sing, sing
which is triple: one, stess, stress, or strummmm, two, three. Triple meter is not always light-hearted.   As I imagine the effect, it must have been like the second movement of the Brahms *Requiem,* the solemn "three-legged" march that accompanies the words "all flesh is as grass.")

Spice for the Anglo-Saxon audience was provided by pithy compounds like *bân-hûs* ("bone-house") for "body," but not for us moderns, whose readings simply do not include them.   This effect can be approximated by using low-frequency "color" words like "hex" or "citadel."

Having said that, however, we can boil all this down thus: we must take what made *Beowulf* sound like poetry to its original audience, and make it sound like the same kind of poetry to the reader of today.   I believe that the best vehicle for this is *terza rima,* the same that got Dante from Hell to Heaven. It is unhurried, seamless, dignified, and it *sounds* like poetry, since it rhymes, although not so obsessively as, say, a greeting card; and the asymmetry of the rhymes does pull the story forward.   It requires more syllables per line, true, but with vigilance no fustian should intrude; and with luck, just maybe there's room for a *Blume* to occasionally become a red, red, rose.

*   *   *

The troop all stood,

Weorod eall aras; 3030.

Then solemnly filed down from Eagles' Hill

leodon unbliðe   under Earnanæs,

While fighting back their tears as best they could.

wollenteare wundur sceawian.

They found there on the sand, lifeless and still,

Fundon ða on sande   sawulleasne

Their chief, bestower of many an arm-band and ring

hlimbed healdan   þone þe him hringas geaf

On them.   They'd witnessed him bravely fulfill

ærran mælum;   þa wæs endedæg 3035.

His destiny, their commander and king,

godum gegongen,   þæt se guðcyning

The Viking prince, who had so strangely died.

Wedra þeoden,   wundordeaðe swealt.

Before, they'd seen a supernatural thing,

ær hi þær gesegan   syllicran wiht,

A monster sprawled out on the other side

wyrm on wonge   wiðerræhtes þær

Rage-contorted, the dragon now lay cold,

laðne licgean;   wæs se legdraca 3040.

Still fearsome, scorch-marks on its glittering hide.

grimlic gryrefah,   gledum beswæle

They paced it off: full fifty feet, all told,

Se wæs fiftiges   fotgemearces

Stretched out before its lair.   It had once soared

lang on legere, lyftwynne heold

Through the night sky, then down would swoop for gold,

nihtes hwilum,   nyðer eft gewat

To seek the deep den where it kept its hoard.

dennes niosian;   wæs ða deaðe fæst, 3045.

In caverns underground it packed its lair

hæfde eorðscrafa   ende genyttod

With golden cups and pitchers that it stored,

Him big stodan   bunan ond orcas,

Platters, once-costly swords strewn here and there,

discas lagon   ond dyre swyrd

Now eaten through with rust, kept underground

omige, þurhetone,   swa hie wið eorðan fæðm

A thousand winters in that musty air.

þusend wintra   þær eardodon.3050.

The trove of heirlooms, mightiest ever found,

þonne wæs þæt yrfe   eacencræftig,

The ancients' gold, was hidden by a spell

iumonna gold   galdre bewunden,

That kept the buried treasure safe and sound,

þæt ðam hringsele   hrinan ne moste

A hex that only God's power could dispel.

gumena ænig,   nefne God sylfa,

The Lord Above alone could grant one's prayer,

sigora Soðcyning,   sealde þam ðe he wolde 3055.

And open the hoard (He's man's Citadel),

he is manna gehyld   hord openian,

But only if man's character is square.

efne swa hwylcum manna,   swa him gemet ðuhte.

A clearly sinful course of action led

XLII   þa wæs gesyne,   þæt se sið ne ðah

The one who'd wrongly hidden in that lair

þam ðe unrihte   inne gehydde

Those ornaments.   The guard earlier killed dead

wræte under wealle.   Weard ær ofsloh 3060.

Some others; a vendetta then broke out,

feara sumne;   þa sio fæhð gewearð

Harshly avenged.   Who knows what lies ahead,

gewrecen wraðlice.   Wundur hwar þonne

What end the valiant man can know about?

eorl ellenrof   ende gefere

The arrival of the day when we depart

lifgesceafta,   þonne leng ne mæg

From family and friends, must be in doubt.

mon mid his magum   meduseld buan. 3065.

Beowulf set out with these thoughts in his heart.

Swa wæs Biowulfe,   þa he biorges weard

Though battle-ready, he knew not at all

sohte, searoniðas;   seolfa ne cuðe

The end he faced.   As for the hex to thwart

þurh hwæt his worulde gedal   weorðan sceolde.

Looting intruders, it guarded the hall

Swa hit oð domes dæg   diope enemdon

Till Doomsday.   The great kings that filled the site

þeodnas mære,   þa ðæt þær dydon, 3070.

With gold ensured that trespassers would fall

þæt se secg wære   synnum scildig

Under a curse, in demon-bonds gripped tight

hergum geheaðerod,   hellbendum fæst,

In agony, for stealing from the hoard.

wommum gewitnad,   se ðone wong strude,

Beowulf was not a man gold could excite;

næfne goldhwæte   gearwor hæfde

He'd viewed it calmly, steadied by the Lord.

Agendes est   ær gesceawod. 3075.

Wiglaf, the son of Wihstan, spoke up then.

Wiglaf maðelode,   Wihstanes sunu:

"The soldier often has to face untoward

Oft sceall eorl monig   anes willan

Events, as sadly happened to us men

wræc adreogan,   swa us geworden is.

When we could not persuade our chieftain dear

Ne meahton we gelæran   leofne þeoden,

The kingdom's shepherd, that it would have been

rices hyrde,   ræd ænigne, 3080.

Too risky to attack the gold-guard, sheer

þæt he ne grette   goldweard þone,

Madness.   Let it lie there where it remained,

lete hyne licgean,   þær he longe wæs,

Inside its cave, until Doomsday draws near.

wicum wunian   oð woruldende;

He still followed his star.   See what we've gained,

Heold on heahgesceap.   hord ys gesceawod,

But at what cost!   Too strong the fate that drove

grimme gegongen;   wæs þæt gifeðe to swið, 3085.

The people's king to charge on, unrestrained.

þe ðone þeodcyning   þyder ontyhte.

I was inside, and looked over the trove,

Ic wæs þær inne   ond þæt eall geondseh,

The hall's rich objects, it was granted me,

recedes geatwa,   þa me gerymed wæs,

Though grudgingly, I was allowed to rove

nealles swæslice   sið alyfed

Down underground.   I grabbed things hastily,

inn under eorðweall.   Ic on ofoste gefeng 3090.

Great handfuls, till I staggered from the weight

micle mid mundum   mægenbyrðenne

Of all that treasure, bore it out where he,

hordgestreona,   hider ut ætbær

My king, still lingered, though he'd met his fate;

cyninge minum.   Cwico wæs þa gena,

Coherent, cogent still, he'd much to say,

wis ond gewittig;   worn eall gespræc

The grave old man ordered me to relate

gomol on gehðo,   ond eowic gretan het, 3095.

That you're to build, when he had passed away,

bæd þæt ge geworhton   æfter wines dædum

At the cremation-place, a towering mound

in bælstede   beorh þone hean,

As he towered over men of his day,

micelne ond mærne,   swa he manna wæs

The worthiest victor in the world around,

wigend weorðfullost   wide geond eorðan,

Enriching his kingdom gloriously.

þenden he burhwelan   brucan moste. 3100.

Let's hurry now, once more, to what he found,

Uton nu efstan   oðre siðe,

And view heaps of exotic jewelry,

seon ond secean   searogimma geþræc,

An underground   marvel!   I'll be your guide,

wundur under wealle;   ic eow wisige,

And bring you to the golden treasury,

þæt ge genoge   neon sceawiað

Thick gold arm-bands.   Prepare the bier outside,

beagas ond brad gold.   Sie sio bær gearo, 3105.

Ready it so, when we emerge, straightway

ædre geæfned,   þonne we ut cymen,

And bear our lord's corpse off with funeral stride

ond þonne geferian   frean userne,

Dear man! — to where we'll reverently lay

leofne mannan,   þær he longe sceal

Him, in the keeping of the Lord, to rest."

on ðæs Waldendes   wære geþolian.

Then Wihstan's son appealed for a display

Het ða gebeodan   byre Wihstanes, 3110.

Of loyalty.   The young hero addressed

hæle hildedior,   hæleða monegum

The nobles, asking them for bonfire-wood.

boldagendra,   þæt hie bælwudu

All, near and far, complied with his request,

feorran feredon,   folcagende,

A fiery funeral for the common good.

godum togenes: Nu sceal gled fretan,

"Let flame consume the warrior-chief laid low!

(weaxan wonna leg)   *wigena strengel,* 3115.

The rain of steel he oftentimes withstood,

þone ðe oft gebad   *isernscure,*

The hail of arrows whizzing from the bow

þonne stræla storm   *strengum gebæded*

Straight shafts that clattered on the shield-wall strong,

scoc ofer scildweall,   *sceft nytte heold,*

Aim-guiding feathers, points that pierce the foe."

Fæðergearwum fus   *flane fulleode*

Indeed, the wise son of Wihstan ere long

Huru se snotra   *sunu Wihstanes* 3120.

Had culled from the late prince's retinue;

acigde of corðre   *cyninges þegnas*

The finest seven of that lordly throng.

syfone tosomne,   *þa selestan,*

This company of eight, all soldiers true,

eode eahta sum   *under inwithrof*

Entered that evil cave.   One, torch in hand,

hilderinca;   *sum on handa bær*

Was leader, with the light to lead them through.

æledleoman,   *se ðe on orde geong.* 3125.

They felt no gold fever.   Calmly the band

Næs ða on hlytme   *hwa þæt hord strude,*

Surveyed the gleaming treasure.   Unprotected,

syððan orwearde   *ænigne dæl*

The spoils of war lay there, at their command.

secgas gesegon   *on sele wunian,*

All junk! they thought, as numbly they collected,

læne licgan;   *lyt ænig mearn*

Then matter-of-factly relayed from the room

> *þæt hi ofostlice   ut geferedon* 3130.

The hard-won gold.   The dragon, disrespected,

> *dyre maðmas;   dracan ec scufun,*

Was dragged away from where it met its doom,

> *wyrm ofer weallclif,   leton weg niman*

Then dumped into the sea, where it fell hard.

> *flod fæðmian   frætwa hyrde.*

Whole wagon-loads of gold came from the tomb,

> *Þa wæs wunden gold   on wæn hladen,*

Great heaps.   The king, borne by his honor-guard

> *æghwæs unrim,   æþeling boren,* 3135.

In state, white-bearded warrior, to Whale's Bluff.

> *har hilderinc   to Hronesnæsse.*

The Vikings held him in such high regard

> *Him ða gegiredan   Geata leode*

That they heaped up a pyre, one grand enough

> *ad on eorðan   unwaclicne,*

For shields to be hung up on either side

> *helmum behongen,   hildebordum,*

Bright armor, helmets too, the battle-stuff

> *beorhtum byrnum,   swa he bena wæs;* 3140.

He'd asked to have around him when he died.

> *alegdon ða tomiddes   mærne þeoden*

The funeral began with loud lament,

> *hæleð hiofende,   hlaford leofne.*

Then greatest of cliff-fires, seen far and wide,

> *Ongunnon þa on beorge   bælfyra mæst*

Was kindled by the guards; up the smoke went

> *wigend weccan;   wudurec astah,*

A swirling black cloud over the flame's roar.

> *sweart ofer swioðole,   swogende leg* 3145.

Up, too, rose shrieks of woe.   When all was spent,

> *wope bewunden   — windblond gelæg —,*

The corpse was smoldering ashes, nothing more,

> *oðþæt he ða banhus   gebrocen hæfde,*

Consumed by fire.   The mourners turned away,

> *hat on hreðre.   Higum unrote*

They grieved and spoke of how things were before.

> *modceare mændon,   mondryhtnes cwealm;*

An old Norse woman sang a funeral lay

> *swylce giomorgyd   sio geomeowle* 3150.

About Beowulf's passing, her hair pulled back,

> *æfter Biowulfe   bundenheorde*

Sang woefully, and then she said her say,

> *song sorgcearig,   sæde geneahhe*

Of how she feared the future: war, attack,

> *þæt hio hyre hearmdagas   hearde ondrede,*

Of slaughtered multitudes, terror, defeats,

> *wælfylla worn,   wigendes egesan,*

Degrading slavery.   Smoke rose skyward, black.

> *hynðo ond hæftnyd.   Heofon rece swealg.* 3155 .

Then on the cliff, to honor their king's feats,

> *Geworhton þa   Wedra leode*

The men heaped up a mound so broad and high,

> *hlæw on hliðe,   se wæs heah ond brad,*

It could be seen by ocean-faring fleets.

> *wægliðendum   wide gesyne,*

To get the mound built, ten whole days went by,

> *ond betimbredon   on tyn dagum*

This tribute to the hero's ashes there.

beadurofes becn,   *bronda lafe* 3160.

They walled it off, to shield it from the eye

wealle beworhton,   *swa hyt weorðlicost*

Of all except those wise beyond compare.

foresnotre men   findan mihton.

On the mound they buried arm-bands and rings,

Hi on beorg dydon   beg ond siglu,

The ornaments once in the dragon's lair.

eall swylce hyrsta,   swylce on horde ær

Inside the cave they'd seized the precious things,

niðhedige men   genumen hæfdon; 3165.

Now the vast fortune's dumped into the earth.

forleton eorla gestreon   eorðan healdan,

Gold in the dirt.   It lies there still, and brings

gold on greote,   þær hit nu gen lifað

No benefits to men.   It has no worth.

eldum swa unnyt   swa hit æror wæs.

About the mound rode a brave cavalcade,

Þa ymbe hlæw riodan   hildediore,

Twelve nobles, princes' sons of noblest birth.

æþelinga bearn,   ealra twelfe, 3170.

The time had come for pageantry, so they'd

woldon care cwiðan,   ond kyning mænan

Assembled to recite their eulogy,

wordgyd wrecan, ond ymb wer sprecan;

His valor and good works their accolade.

eahtodan eorlscipe ond his ellenweorc

His manly deeds they praised, as it should be,

duguðum demdon, — swa hit gedefe bið,

It's fitting that men praise their absent friend,

> *þæt mon his winedryhten   wordum herge,* 3175.

Whose heartfelt love should last unendingly,

> *ferhðum freoge,   þonne he forð scile*

When his life finally comes to its end.

> *of lichaman   læded weorðan.*

The Vikings kept on lamenting for days

> *Swa begnornodon   Geata leode*

Their lord's death, and his close friends would commend

> *hlafordes hryre,   heorðgeneatas,*

Him as better than other kings, in ways

> *cwædon þæt he wære   wyruldcyninga* 3180.

That showed his mildness, gentleness; he would

> *manna mildest   ond monðwærust,*

Be kindest to men, eagerest for their praise.

> *leodum liðost   ond lofgeornost.*

Anonymity as a Rationalization:

Shakespeare's *Titus Andronicus*

Performing Shakespeare's *Titus Andronicus* is all in a day's work for today's actors, directors and production crews; it is the theater's fourth estate, the audience, that will find the play difficult. We Shakespeare-loving theatergoers have certain expectations: the purchase price of our ticket entitles us to resent self-indulgent actors and self-important directors, but *Titus* leaves us with the feeling that we have been betrayed by the playwright. We ask for bread, and the Swan of Avon gives us a stone: instead of interesting dialogue, memorable characters and intriguing plots, we find ourselves watching a tiresome hodgepodge of sadism and rant. *Titus,* put simply, seems disappointingly un-Shakespearean.

This chapter will argue that *Titus Andronicus* has a rightful place in the Shakespeare canon and in the Shakespeare repertory, as a juvenile work of period interest, that may be performed unapologetically, and performed uncut.

I trust that the connoisseur will indulge a synopsis of the drama's plot. Not everyone has read *Titus,* and I had rather include readers than exclude them. Titus Andronicus is a victorious Roman general who has returned with Gothic captives. He sacrifices a son of Tamora, the queen of the Goths, despite

her pleas.   He is then called to arbitrate between rival claimants
to the "empery," a quaint old word for the throne.   The man he
chooses abruptly falls in love with Tamora.   Tamora has a lover,
a Moor named Aaron, who urges her two remaining sons to
murder Titus' son-in-law and rape his daughter.   They do so,
and also cut off her hands and cut out her tongue.   Aaron
frames two of Titus' remaining sons for the murder.   Aaron
informs Titus that the emperor will pardon the sons in exchange
for the amputation of a hand.   This proves to be a lie, and Titus
vows revenge, sending his remaining son to lead the Goths
against Rome.   Tamora gives birth to a black baby.   Titus kills
Tamora's two sons and makes pies of their flesh, then feeds
them to their mother and the emperor.   He kills his daughter,
then kills Tamora; the emperor kills him, then Titus' son kills
the emperor and Aaron, and is proclaimed emperor himself.
Murray's phrase is "darkest Shakespeare,"[1] although Edward
Ravenscroft, in his Restoration adaptation of *Titus Andronicus,*
added dialogue (which I give in modern spelling and
punctuation) that is darker still: in his version, Tamora kills
her own baby.   The villain seems at first to accept that he has
been upstaged.

> *Aaron.*   She has outdone me in my own art,
> Outdone me in murder.   Killed her own child.

Yet the Moor is not to be outdone, after all: he rallies himself
to direct a final soupçon of darkness at the dark child's corpse:

---

[1]   Murray 2001, 111.

Give it me – I'll eat it![2]

This chapter will alternate between an examination of the long critical tradition involving *Titus Andronicus* and an examination of a modern production, performed in October 2006 in the small rural school district of Sadler and Southmayde (S&S), just north of Dallas, Texas, USA.   It could be said that the director's approach was eclectic: the director and the composer of the incidental music wanted a lot of drumming between the scenes and during the violent episodes, so an enormous Japanese-style hanging drum, bright red, dominated the stage.   It could be said that the director's approach was realistic: to achieve the necessary gruesomeness, a fake hand and two fake heads were obtained from a nearby school of nursing, and the fake blood, although so messy that the stage had to be repainted three times, was visually convincing.   The director made cuts, like the majority of modern directors, with predictably mixed results: cutting the fly-killing scene tightened up the play's momentum, since that scene is a digression, but on the other hand, it is not a bad digression; cutting the business of Aaron's baby deprived the Moor of some of his best lines, but on the other hand, it avoided the distracting absurdity of the playwright's assigning to Tamora the gestation period of a field mouse.   The "mobs" of senators and soldiers were cut, which recalled the appendix to Hughes' edition, where that editor shows how Titus can be performed with only fourteen actors.   (Hughes 162)   I chose this student production for observation out of necessity: learnèd commentary on professional performances of

---

[2]   Ravenscroft 55.

Titus, from Peter Brook's famous 1955 staging on, is so uniformly New Age that it is simply unusable.   Another reason I chose this production is because I had access to a great deal of behind-the-scenes information and was able to videorecord lengthy interviews with four of the principals, since they are, as we say in Texas, kinfolks.   The director is my brother Jon Skupin, and the composer/assistant director is my sister-in-law Annette.   The cast included my nieces Becca (as Marcus in a trousers role) and Katy (who doubled in no fewer than four minor roles; in a small school one has to "make do").   Far from the madding crowd, at S&S the issues facing the actors and audience are observable, to use an old expression, *de novo*:   as if they were new.   To deal with these interpretive questions, however, it is useful to back up a bit.

There are several senses in which *Titus Andronicus* is a new play: new, because *Titus* lacks the superstructure of criticism that Shakespeare's other plays have elicited, not because no one has commented on the play, but because much of that superstructure has collapsed in recent years, which means that, instead of an orderly exposition of knowns, commentary on the play must begin with a list of items that were once certain, but are now uncertain.   Time was when no discussion of *Titus* was complete without a disquisition on the Peacham Drawing, introduced to the scholarly community by E. K. Chambers in 1925.[3]   This pen and ink sketch shows a row of figures in theatrical poses followed by some forty lines from Shakespeare's tragedy.   The date is hard to read, but is generally understood to be 1595.   The placement of the figures does not match any

---

[3]   Chambers 1925, 326.

scene in the play, and this discrepancy was the subject of decades of speculation until 1999, when June Schlueter proposed that the drawing represents a scene from a different Titus, preserved in German in a volume of plays performed on the Continent by touring English actors.[4] Her rereading of the Peacham Drawing is now taken to be definitive. Yet her discussion reminds the reader of an important cautionary variable: in addition to the German Titus (and a later Dutch *Aran en Titus* ["Aaron and Titus"]), the diary of impresario Philip Henslowe records not only a *Titus and Vespasian* in 1592 (which may or may not be the same as a *"tittus & vespacia"* from that same year), but also a *"titus & ondronicus"* performed by the Earl of Sussex's Men in January 1594, and an *"andronicus"* performed by the Lord Admiral's and/or Lord Chamberlain's Men in June 1594.[5] This is the House of Mirrors, and should warn the reader to tread carefully in matters of date; on the other hand, knowledge of the uncertainties of the question allows the reader to approach Shakespeare's tragedy as it stands on the page, without preconceptions: *de novo*: as if it were new.

Titus Andronicus is new in another, more important sense: although it was a repertory piece on the Elizabethan[6] and Restoration stage,[7] in Victorian and twentieth-century theaters *Titus* was seldom performed or filmed until the surge of interest we have seen in the last few years: this means that for much of its modern history the drama has existed not in the memory of

---

[4] Schlueter 172.
[5] Schlueter 176.
[6] Massai 7.
[7] van Lennep 273, 352.

audiences, but in the mind's eye of readers, and this is not at all the way that drama is to be experienced.   A play is not a play until it is onstage.

The third sense in which *Titus* is new is because it has long been proposed as an example of a new way of looking at Shakespeare, not only as author, but as co-author.   More accurately, Shakespeare as collaborator is an old idea that has only recently become acceptable and accepted; the earliest statement of the idea dates from 1687, in Ravenscroft's preface to his adaptation of the play.   It is instructive to note the various ways that Ravenscroft's allegation has been treated over the years, from bland acceptance[8] to flat rejection[9] to detailed, energetic rebuttal.[10]   Be that as it may, this Restoration writer's statement has never been central to the question; commentators have instead focused on the play's internals, leading to an extensive scholarly debate, especially during the "disintegrationist" years around the turn of the twentieth century, when *Titus Andronicus* was treated as a wedge against the First Folio: if a case against sole Shakespearean authorship could be made with *Titus,* this conclusion could be generalized against other plays in the canon. J. M. Robertson's *Introduction to the Study of the Shakespeare Canon* exemplifies this line of attack.   Dover Wilson goes so far as to call it "the first battering-ram in a grand assault upon the integrity of the First Folio."[11]   Robertson's 1924 study is actually an amplification of work that first appeared in 1903. In 1904 we find an example of counterattack that is of period

---

[8]   Gollancz vi
[9]   Crawford 110.
[10]   Murray 2005, xxviii.
[11]   Wilson xv.

interest, where the Arden editor rhapsodizes that *Titus* is self-evidently Shakespearean, since it is a companion-piece to, of all things, *A Midsummer Night's Dream*: " ...just as a piece of tapestry or carpet presents the *same* design on both its sides in *reversed colours*," he presents Aaron as an anti-Puck, the emperor Saturninus as an anti-Theseus, and so on down the line, even maintaining that "Titania's temporary infatuation for Bottom has its tragic counterpart in Tamora's passion for Aaron."[12]   Leaving this blood-from-a-stone reading "with a famous remark of Puck's in our ears,"[13] we find that later writers would have no need to grasp at straws in this way: the victory of the Shakespeare fundamentalists was complete, so complete that Paul Bertram, in his 1965 *Shakespeare and the Two Noble Kinsmen* (which argued for the canonization of *Kinsmen* by process of elimination, by "bumping" Fletcher from his status as co-author), prefaced his book with a defensive, "Any book that sets out to extend the limits of the Shakespeare canon is bound to engender suspicion."[14]   Times have changed: at the beginning of the twenty-first century the mood of Shakespeareans is unapologetic, confident enough to consider the possibility of other hands in the lesser plays; it is even expansionist, and talk of the annexation of formerly doubtful plays like *The Two Noble Kinsmen* and *Edward III* is now quite acceptable.

Let us not get ahead of ourselves, however.   "Disintegrationism" was in the air at the turn of the twentieth century, and it was destructive and anti-Bard.   Our consciousness of this controversy

---

[12] Baildon lxvi.
[13] Ridley xii.
[14] Bertram ix.

will excuse apparent inconsistencies in scholars of that era.   In 1900 the *Jahrbuch der Deutschen Shakespeare-Gesellschaft* ("yearbook of the German Shakespeare Society") published Charles Crawford's "The Date and Authenticity of Titus Andronicus," in which that author rejects the idea that Shakespeare collaborated with his contemporary George Peele (1556-96), but then proceeds to give evidence that The Bard did just that.   This frequently-cited, but frequently-misquoted article is a good introduction to the way that humdrum matters of date and authorship have been reassessed *de novo* in the past few years.   Crawford was right to begin with Francis Meres' well-known mention of *Titus* in 1598, of which more later; his comparisons with Peele's poem on the Order of the Garter are interesting; but he goes too far with his attempt to hyperfinesse the date of *Titus* ("Now to the proof, which hinges on the question of date."[15]   Crawford was only one of many critics (including Schlueter) who based their arguments on the broken reed of Henslowe's diary, falling into what I will call the "ne" trap.   It used to be a critical commonplace to interpret "ne," found written next to *Titus* in 1594, as an abbreviation for "new."   (To his credit, Chambers had his doubts.[16])   In 1991 Winifred Frazer demonstrated that this interpretation was unlikely ("ne" being found next to the names of plays that were demonstrably not new), and that "ne" probably refers to performances in the theater at Newington Butts.[17]

The value of Crawford's article does not, however, hinge on the question of date.   (Nor should it be diminished by the

---

[15] Crawford 112
[16] Chambers 1988:1 320.
[17] Frazer 35.

fact that Baildon's "colours reversed" fantasy, above, had its origins in an earlier Crawford piece.) Crawford was ahead of his time in the collecting of similarities between passages in *Titus Andronicus* and the poetry of George Peele. We may smile at Crawford's out-of-hand rejection of a collaboration between the two playwrights despite his own evidence to the contrary,[18] and we may be moved to waggery as to who was stealing from whom, and how, but the case for joint authorship with Peele is a question that will not go away. Brian Vickers' recent *Shakespeare, Co-author* proposes not only *Titus,* but four other plays (*Timon of Athens, Pericles, Henry VIII* and *The Two Noble Kinsmen*) as joint efforts (reinstating Fletcher in *Kinsmen, pace* Bertram), which shows just how much the idea of collaboration is in the air these days.[19] Vickers' evidence is impressive (although he still does not show who was stealing from whom, and how), and the last four of his candidates should be taken seriously; in the case of *Titus,* however, we must be wary of the word "co-author," since that term conjures up a mental picture of two playwrights meeting, say, at the Mermaid Tavern, briskly shaking hands, removing their doublets and getting down to business. I maintain that *Titus* is an apprentice piece, and, since apprentices do not deal as equals with masters, it is more likely that young Shakespeare acquired his raw material either by burning the midnight oil or by employing his incomparable ear during live performances. *Titus's* Aaron speaks of a fellow Moor named Muly (4.2.153), and there are no fewer than three Moors named Muly in Peele's *Battle of Alcazar,*

---

[18] Crawford 109.
[19] Vickers *passim.*

but there are any number of scenarios that would explain this overlap: Peele may not have learned of the "collaboration" until *Titus Andronicus* received its premiere, assuming that he ever did.

Be that as it may, it is a relief to find that the twenty-first century reader is comfortable with the idea that Shakespeare had other collaborators besides Fletcher. For years I wondered about *Pericles*, but repressed my opinions, because back in the nineteen-seventies such ideas seemed *lèse majesté*.

I hasten to insist that Peele not be denied *majesté* of his own. It will not do to use Peele as a fig leaf, that is, to say that if a passage in *Titus* is flat, or contrived, or silly, then Peele is to blame. He wrote entertaining plays, good poetry in English, and Latin verse that was very, very correct. Peele was no slouch.

Nor was Robert Greene a slouch (his hand in *Titus* had been argued four years before Crawford's article appeared[20]); nor was Thomas Kyd or Thomas Dekker or Christopher Marlowe, to mention other contemporaries of Shakespeare. Yet there has been no rush to perform Greene's *Selimus,* or Kyd's *Spanish Tragedy,* or Dekker's *Shoemaker's Holiday,* or Marlowe's *Dido,* despite their respective superiority over *Titus Andronicus* in quality of poetry, fullness of characterization, momentum of plot, or trendiness (the opening scene of *Dido* is expressly and overtly man-boy homosexual). *Titus* lives, or perhaps we should say will not die, because it is attributed to Shakespeare, and our times are hungry for Shakespeare the author, and intrigued by Shakespeare the man. Our times are not hungry for George Peele, the author or the man, or for any of the other playwrights I

---

[20] Greene xx

have just mentioned; without Shakespearean authorship, *Titus* would attract no more commentary than Greene's *Selimus,* and would be seen no more frequently on the boards than Peele's *Battle of Alcazar.* Still, the attribution to The Bard is not just marketing: I have mentioned Meres' attribution in passing, in the context of Crawford's article, but his comments are worth a closer look. First, however, a look at another famous Meres passage:

> ...so the sweete wittie soule of *Ouid* liues in mellifluous & hony-tongued *Shakespeare,* witnes his *Venus and Adonis,* his *Lucrece,* his sugred Sonnets among his priuate friends &c.[21]

This excerpt is worth recalling because it enhances Meres' credibility: if the Sonnets were as yet unpublished, then Meres could not have known about them unless he was some sort of insider, either an acquaintance of one of Shakespeare's "priuate friends" or a "priuate friend" himself. Now to the attribution proper:

> As *Plautus* and *Seneca* are accounted the best for Comedy and Tragedy among the Latines: so *Shakespeare* among the English is the most excellent in both kinds for the stage; for Comedy, witnes his *Gentlemen of Verona,* his *Errors,* his *Loue labors lost,* his *Loue labours wonne,* his *Midsummers night dreame* & his *Merchant of*

---

[21] Chambers 1988:2 194.

Venice: for Tragedy his *Richard the 2. Richard the 3. Henry the 4. King John, Titus Andronicus* and his *Romeo* and *Iuliet.*[22]

It must be admitted that *Titus* is in good company here.   Yet it is worth stressing that only *Titus* has a tradition of disputed authorship.   I know of no one who has proposed claimants for the authorship of great masterpieces like *Romeo and Juliet* and *Richard III.*   Scholars have long been comfortable with joint authorship of *Titus* for the very subjective reason that they have long been uncomfortable with the idea that the drama is the work of William Shakespeare: they want to unload it.

The general tenor of the argument against The Bard's authorship involves what I will call "horribilism," a term from the 1930's which means that the play moves forward not by the plausible working-out of a plot, but by a series of shocks, and frequently jejune shocks.   This technique is sometimes effective in a stopgap sort of way, as in Greene's *Selimus,* where a flagging scene is spiced up by having a harmless old man's eyes gouged out and his hands cut off (1417ff), but a little of this goes a long way: if overused, horribilism can misfire: the New Temple editor of *Titus* opined that "the horrors that are designed to make our blood run cold are so crude that they are more calculated to make us smile."[23]   Or worse: the reader familiar with reviews of modern performances of *Titus* will have noted their preoccupation with the ingenious techniques used by earnest New Age directors to prevent audiences from bursting

---

[22] Chambers 1988:2 194.
[23] Ridley x.

out laughing during the performances. Those who dislike the play may wish to rest their case right there, but a closer look at the matter will prompt an interesting and relevant question: Does Shakespeare want us to laugh? There is one critical tradition that maintains that he does, that *Titus Andronicus* is a satire, a light-hearted romp at the expense of Shakespeare's rivals. I admit that this is a reading with a respectable pedigree: Back in 1934 Wilson wrote, "Once catch the trick of it, you can see [Shakespeare] laughing behind his hand through most of the scenes he rehandled,"[24] and this theory still had its adherents in the year 2007, at S&S, where the assistant director/composer was of this opinion, as I found during an interview. This understanding, however, assumes that Shakespeare had reached his artistic maturity when he wrote *Titus*; there is abundant evidence, however, to show that the play is a juvenile work. Even by reclassifying the play as a parody, though, *Titus* would still fail, since parody is not effective unless the writer can outdo his original, and there are parameters in which *Titus* is quite amateurish, far inferior to the standards of Peele, Greene and the rest of the "horribilist" pack, so I respectfully disagree with my sister-in-law and all others who take *Titus* to be a skillful satire.

The S&S director, on the other hand, e-mailed me that he took it for granted that the audience would laugh, not with The Bard, but at him, because Shakespeare "jumped the shark." When I confessed my ignorance of this bit of theater slang, he sent a definition from wikipedia:

> **Jumping the shark** is a metaphor for the tipping point at which a TV series passes its peak or introduces plot

---

[24] Wilson li.

twists which are inconsistent with what has preceded them. Once a show has jumped the shark, the viewer senses a noticeable decline in quality or feels the show has undergone too many changes to retain its original charm.

He then explained how he applied it to *Titus Andronicus*:

It also implies that the writer/director has broken faith with the audience. For TITUS, bringing on those heads and the chopped off hand... Lavinia bearing the hand away in her mouth?? The shark is jumped.   As a director the rest of the show is damage control![25]

This was before the performances; afterwards, he was of the opinion that another,   even larger shark is jumped in Act V, scene 2, where the playwright commits the second-worst of thespian sins, asking the actor to do his work for him.   Tamora says that Titus is insane, and Titus says that he is pretending to be insane, but I can find nothing in his lines that convey either state.   The actor is on his own; the S&S students got through the scene, but no thanks to the playwright.

A similar thespian sin is asking the audience to do the playwright's work for him, as in the case of disentangling the two Cornelias.   Shakespeare names the offstage midwife, "Cornelia," (4.2.143), evidently forgetting that in the previous scene he has already used the name (4.1.12) for a different offstage figure.   Bate helpfully identifies the first Cornelia as a

---

[25] Skupin, personal communication.

figure from Roman legend,[26] but is curiously non-judgmental about the careless, confusing repetition of the name, merely remarking that "In seeking a Roman name for the midwife, Shakespeare's mind went back 4.1.12," as if this sort of muddle were the most natural, most Shakespearean of devices.

Another dramaturgical sin is when the playwright distracts the audience by writing nonsense.   In the same scene where the playwright has carelessly introduced his second Cornelia, the audience must wrestle with the matter of the birth of Tamora's black baby after an impossibly brief pregnancy.   Trumpets announce that the emperor has a son, which implies that the baby has been inspected closely enough for it to be identified as a boy, but not, we infer, so closely as to be identified as black, since Aaron assures us that this detail can be swept under the rug with a murder or two.   (Will he also kill the trumpeters?)   It is hard to imagine Shakespeare working at cross-purposes this way, distracting his audience with shticks that clash with life experience.

It is by now obvious to the reader that I reject absolutely the protestations of *Titus'* modern shills, who argue that the play is a masterpiece that is not given a fair hearing because modern critics are un-hep and modern audiences are squares.   Vickers, for instance, asserts that

These doubts about Shakespeare's authorship had no scholarly basis, external or internal, but expressed an aesthetico-ethical dislike for the violence and corporeal mutilations that take place both on and off stage.   Any attentive and unprejudiced

---

[26] Bate 211.

reading of the play could show that the violence is in no way gratuitous...[27] (Vickers 150)

Fiddlesticks!   Theatrical violence is always gratuitous: Othello could have simply gotten a divorce.   It is disingenuous to claim that *Titus'* violence *per se* is the problem.   The modern theatergoer has the mental toughness to observe with nary a tremor the shedding of fake blood onstage (or even to be spattered with fake blood, as were some of the front-row spectators in the S&S production), and the modern moviegoer has long been Stoic when viewing the lifelike mishaps of Hollywood stunt men. The problem for modern audiences with *Titus* is its ratio of cruelties to theatrical worth: a bucket of blood for an inch of plot is not a good bargain.   Vickers later laments that "it is disappointing to find contemporary scholars continuing to dismiss the play on unexamined aesthetico-ethical grounds." [28]   In other words, modern critics are un-hep. Vickers offers no opinion as to whether or not modern audiences are also slaves to these "aesthetico-ethical" considerations; I hope they are.   I am, and hope never to be emancipated. Awkwardly for *Titus*-touts, Peter Brook, the object of much praise for his 1955 revival of the play, is on record as being equally un-hep, in his "Open Letter to William Shakespeare."

> When the notices of Titus Andronicus came out, giving us full marks for saving your dreadful play, I could not help feeling a twinge of guilt.   For to tell the truth it had not occurred to any of us in rehearsal that the play was so bad.[29]

---

[27] Vickers 150.
[28] Vickers 151.
[29] Brook 72.

At the beginning of this essay I said that performing *Titus* is all in a day's work for today's actors and directors; evidently Brook and his cast would have disagreed.

Make no mistake about it: *Titus Andronicus* is a dud. I am not speaking of any comparison with *Hamlet*; it will not even stand comparison with the better plays of Peele (or Greene, or the pack). Was *Titus* popular with Elizabethan and Restoration audiences? So was bearbaiting. The modern theatergoer will be curious about *Titus* only insofar as it gives him a glimpse of The Bard on a bad day.

And The Bard's play it is. I regard Meres' attribution to Shakespeare as the question's evidentiary vanishing point (apart, of course, from the testimony of the First Folio); this or that evidence may support this or that scenario, but a scenario is not proof. It will be seen that comparison between the styles of Peele's works and *Titus* is fruitful, but we must be cautious: the "crit" also has Marlowe, Kyd, Greene, and Lodge waiting in the wings as plausible co-authors. (Robertson, *passim*) Metz even mentions Thomas Nashe, although he decides against that candidate.[30] Yet it is not only in order to head off an authorial *Sorcerer's Apprentice,* or to avoid a scenario where *Titus* was written by some sort of blue-ribbon panel, that I propose that Meres' attribution be considered the evidentiary vanishing point; nor is it because studies involving similarities between words and phrases found in *Titus* with words and phrases found in Peele (or Greene, or the pack) do not always take into account their similarities with words and phrases found in William Shakespeare.

---

[30] Metz 248.

The way to determine the date and authorship of *Titus Andronicus* is by considering elements in the play that have no similarity with the style of William Shakespeare at all. The matter, as Crawford would say, hinges on date; Ridley formulated the question more precisely: "Where in Shakespeare's dramatic career do we feel that we can reasonably put this play?"[31] Once an accurate dating of *Titus* has been established, it will be seen that sole Shakespearean authorship is not inconsistent with resemblances to the writings of other playwrights or with *Titus'* amateurishness. Establishing Shakespearean authorship of *Titus Andronicus*, for good or ill, begins, paradoxically, by considering details of plot and dialogue that seem at first glance to militate against Shakespearean authorship.

The greatest dramaturgical sin a playwright can commit is to write dialogue that undercuts what the actor is supposed to portray. Shakespeare sets up Titus before his entrance as noble (1.1.25 and 1.1.50), good (1.1.37 and 1.1.64), "patron of virtue" (1.1.65), the thoughtful, dispassionate arbiter whom all trust; then after his entrance Titus is portrayed as barking mad. When Titus' son blocks his way, instead of saying something reasonable, like, "Step aside," Titus kills the boy (1.1.292). Good? Noble? Titus orders that Tamora's son be sacrificed; he hears her plea for mercy and her vow of vengeance; then he speaks of his hope that, having become empress, she will be, of all things, grateful to him.

> *Marcus.* How comes it that the subtle Queen of Goths
> Is of a sudden thus advanced in Rome?

---

[31] Ridley ix.

Titus.   I know not, Marcus, but I know it is,
(Whether by device or no, the heavens can tell.)
Is she not then beholding to the man
That brought her for this high good turn so far?
Yes, and will nobly him remunerate.   (1.1.391-8)

Remunerate!   It sounds as if Titus is expecting a tip.   If Titus is supposed to feign insanity at the end of the play, then the author must establish the protagonist's sanity at the beginning. Instead, we have the opposite: Shakespeare assigns to Titus actions and dialogue that are prima facie delusional in the opening scene, when he is supposed to be sane.

Titus is also prima facie gullible in the matter of cutting off his own hand, although Shakespeare spreads the gullibility around: Marcus and Lucius also take Aaron at his word when the Moor announces that Titus' two sons will be pardoned if somebody sends the emperor a severed hand.   Up to this point the dramatist has written nothing to portray these characters as credulous, so all three must fall out of character to enact the preposterous three-way scramble to be the first to amputate, based merely on Aaron's say-so.   Is this scene consistent with our knowledge of Shakespeare the peerless observer of human nature, the supreme craftsman of plot?   Certainly not, but with a little patience we will see that the thread of callowness that runs through *Titus* from beginning to end need not be a bar to Shakespearean authorship.

For over a hundred years scholars have produced vocabulary studies of *Titus Andronicus*.   The reader is welcome to trudge through them, but I can sum up the question thus: about half of them prove that Shakespeare wrote *Titus*, and about half of them prove that he did not. All of them, however, prove that Shakespeare was not writing in a vacuum. I offer the results of an informal and unsystematic survey of my own. In Marlowe's *Dido* we find hands cut off (2.1.242) and ravishment (2.1.275), and both acts are gratuitous, since they are found in a speech based on the second book of the *Aeneid,* although neither act of violence is in Virgil. I find the words "hurly-burly," "winter's tale" (twice), and "out of joint" (three times). I have already cited the eye-gouging and amputations in Greene's *Selimus,* but there is also "picking and stealing" (1983), an innocent girl pleading for her life à la Lavinia (1416), atheism à la Aaron (340, 4295), and the quaint old word "empery" no fewer than six times (608, 759, 925, 983, 1736, 2360). In Kyd's *Spanish Tragedy* the hero bites his own tongue off (4.4.191), and there is a passage (3.11.30) that mirrors Titus' much-admired "Ha, ha, ha!" (3.1.265), although Kyd has nine "ha's" to Shakespeare's three. (Kyd may have the edge in quantity of interjections, but Shakespeare leads in variety, with Titus's "O, O, O" [3.2.68] and Aaron's "Wheak, wheak! / So cries a pig preparèd for the spit." [4.2.128]). In *The Spanish Tragedy* there is also "labour's lost" and "naked bed" à la *Venus and Adonis* (twice). In the introduction we find Revenge personified, which recalls Act V, scene 2 of *Titus,* and in Kyd's 2.4.87 a sword used as a cross on which a vow of secrecy is sworn. Peele's *Arraignment of Paris* even has a "stricken deer" (3.1.29).

In Peele's *Edward I* there is a quotation from Horace (1.170), which recalls yet another jejune passage in *Titus:* on hearing the opening lines of Horace's *Odes* I.22, Chiron exclaims:

> *Chiron.*   O, 'tis a verse in Horace; I know it well:
> I read it in the grammar long ago.

Evidently it has slipped the playwright's mind that he has made Chiron a Goth, and that he has set that nation up as "barbarous." (1.1.28)   Reading Horace in a Gothic grammar school?   On the subject of Latin, the quotation from Ovid (*Metamorphoses* 1.150), "Terras Astræa reliquit" ("the goddess of justice, Astraea, has left the earth") in *Titus* (4.3.4) has a parallel in the title of Peele's pageant *Descensus Astræae* ("the descent of Astraea").

There is one area, however, in which *Titus* stands apart from its rivals: the inferiority of its poetry.   I am not speaking subjectively, of snippets that happen to set my teeth on edge, like

> *Titus.*   Mark, Marcus, mark!   (3.1.43)

There are rhymes that are self-evidently jarring, as witness the tragedy's grating final couplet.

> *Lucius.*   Her life was beastly and devoid of pity,
> And being dead, let birds on her take pity. (5.3.199-200).

What an anticlimax!   "Pity" rhyming with "pity!"   Nor is this the only homonymic "clunker."   By whom is Lavinia surprised?

> *Bassianus.*   By him that justly may
> Bear his betrothed from all the world away.
> *Mutius.*   Brothers, help to convey her hence away. (1.1.287-9)

This tops the previous example: note how "may" and "convey" draw attention to the flat repetition of "away."   The next example, though, tops this one.   What does the Moor Aaron have to say about his baby?

> *Aaron.*   Coal black is better than another hue,

In that it scorns to bear another hue.   (4.2.99-100)

Not just "hue," but "another hue" is repeated.   Finally, observe how jingle-jangle can undercut onstage mayhem.

> *Saturninus.*   Die, frantic wretch, for this accursèd deed.
> [*kills Titus*]
> *Lucius.*   Can the son's eye behold his father bleed?
> There's meed for meed, death for a deadly deed. [*kills Saturninus*]

O mighty Caesar, dost thou lie so low?   It will not do to fob these passages off on, say, Robert Greene; they are, on the contrary, arguments against Greene's authorship, since in the *Selimus* I have mentioned he employs a very strict rhyme scheme for most of the drama without veering into anything like *Titus'* cacophony at all.

Peele, it must be admitted, is not completely absolved.   In *Edward I* he writes

> *Joan.*   My king, my king, let Fortune have her course: —
> Fly thou, my soul, and take a better course.
> (24.199-200)

(These lines would be scarcely noticed though, overshadowed as they are by the astonishing anachronism that that precedes them, where King Edward quotes from Ariosto's *Orlando Furioso*, a poem not written until some two centuries after His Majesty died.)   In *The Arraignment of Paris* we find

> *Faunus.*   There's no such matter, Pan; we are all friends assembled hither,
> To bid Queen Juno and her pheers most humbly welcome hither. (1.1.19-20)

but this hither-hither is the only instance I find there.   (Peele's editor[32] glosses "pheeres" as "companions.)   In another note on the same page, commenting on a line that should be iambic hexameter,

> *Pan.*   Peace, man, for shame!   shalt have both lambs and dams and flocks and herds and all, (1.1.17)

the editor writes, "A very long line; but I fail to see that any words can be discarded."

Titus Andronicus has its share of very long lines as well, not to mention some very short ones, but it is not necessary to add the evidence of rhythm to the evidence of rhyme and reason: I think that I have demonstrated sufficiently that some of *Titus'* poetry is not just sub-Shakespearean, but just plain bad, and this is added to passages I have cited where The Bard, the supreme observer of human nature, appears to have no knowledge of human nature at all.   This leads to a choice: either the playwright was negligent, or the playwright was a naif with a tin ear.   It will not do to argue negligence, because it is haste that makes waste, and the publication time line of *Titus* shows no haste at all: the first of three quartos was published in 1594,[33]

---

[32] Peele 8.
[33] Witherspoon 115.

which would have left our author twenty-two years to retouch these impossibly unharmonious lines, yet he did not do it. We know that he did revise the play, because in the First Folio there is an extra scene, the fly-killing scene, but that is the only change that was made.

Having eliminated negligence, we are left with callowness and a tin ear. At first glance it may seem preposterous that the author of *Romeo and Juliet* had no ear for poetry, or that the author of *Richard III* had no life experience, but let us go slowly. Why does this dilemma exist? Because *Titus Andronicus* is regarded as being contemporaneous with Shakespeare plays that are indisputably great. Let us recall, however, that this chronology was based on a faulty understanding of Henslow's "ne." Once this error is removed, the date for *Titus Andronicus* goes into free-fall, and we are left with the play as it stands on the page, and as it plays on the stage. Based on the internals of the play, my conclusion is this: William Shakespeare wrote *Titus Andronicus* before he wrote anything else.

The operative word in this dictum is "anything," and here it is useful to recall the expansion of the Shakespeare canon that has occurred in recent years. From *Titus* to *Richard III* is an impossible leap, but the leap from *Titus* to *Edward III* is not so hard to accept, and *Titus-Edward III-Richard III* is a plausible line of development. Including formerly non-canonical plays in the question also provides external evidence, although of a sliding nature: when was *The Two Noble Kinsmen* written? Well, *Titus Andronicus* was written before that. The same goes for *Edward III*: *Titus* was written before that, and on and on. Each new play or collaboration that is dated pushes the date of *Titus* back just that far, on the grounds of *Titus'* immaturity. If we allow for Peele-inspired retouches before the 1594 quarto was published, I would maintain that it is not unreasonable to posit that the bulk of *Titus* was written in 1583.   No one, I think, would have a problem imagining Shakespeare having a tin ear at the age of nineteen, or, to put it more gracefully, lacking the auditory sensitivity that the mature Swan of Avon would consistently show; no one would have a problem imagining a teen-age playwright writing naive passages; and no one should have a problem assuming that *Titus* gathered dust until after the young playwright got his show-business break, possibly with the likes of *Romeo and Juliet* and *Richard III,* since it is unreasonable to assume that Shakespeare got his show-business break immediately on arriving in London, and since, in any case, the date of a play's composition need have nothing to do with the date of a play's premiere or publication.   (Peele's *David and Bethsabe* and *Sir Clyomon and Sir Clamydes* were both published in 1599, and as we know, Peele died in 1596.)   The premiere of *Titus Andronicus* evidently came at the right moment, since it was a box-office hit, and show business is, after all, a business.   This success would justify the drama's inclusion in the First Folio, and would also explain the author's reluctance to tinker with the play, other than adding a new scene (a cuttable scene, since it does not advance the plot):   why spoil a commercial success by making it arty?   Why reboil old bones?

I began this article by saying that the problems with the rehabilitation of *Titus Andronicus* are related to the audience. "The drama's laws the drama's patrons give / For we who live to please must please to live," wrote Garrick; and musicians will recall the pithy, homely maxim, "If they didn't applaud, it means you played the wrong number."   It will not do to promote *Titus Andronicus* as a cool, campy predecessor of *The Rocky Horror Picture Show.*   The modern theatergoer knows flim-flam.   Yet a modern audience (barring the intrusions of self-indulgent actors and self-important directors) should have no problem sitting through a performance of *Titus,* if it is presented as a look over young Shakespeare's shoulder, and as a preview of what was to come: Aaron as an anti-Puck will not sell any tickets, but Aaron as a proto-Iago just might.   Truth in advertising allows for tact in advertising: in the production at S&S, the audience's expectations had been based on performances of seven of Shakespeare's mainstream plays; indeed, the director's signature piece was *A Midsummer Night's Dream.*   Also, the audience was mentally connected to the performance in a way unimaginable in a production involving anonymous professionals: the actors were playing to doting parents and grandparents, and to schoolmates, and were required to enact murder, rape and cannibalism, an uncomfortable situation for all concerned.   The director prepared the audience for the production by calling *Titus* "our Halloween play," and in fact scheduled one performance on Halloween Night.   He warned the actors to be braced for laughter, although there was, as we have noted, an honest difference of opinion as to why the audience would laugh.

Going from the specific to the general, much of the confusion about *Titus Andronicus* is resolved by establishing its genre.   Referring to *Titus* as a "tragedy of blood" will lead us astray: the tragedy of blood is impelled by the inexorable logic of cause and effect.   We need another term, and the term I have revived, horribilism, is as good as any.   *Titus* is a tragedy of horribilism, and in a tragedy of horribilism the plot moves forward by shocks, frequently brainless shocks. *Titus Andronicus* is structured like a bullfight, dragging the audience along by cumulative cruelties. Should the reader object that the reference to modern bullfighting is anachronistic, I will gladly substitute bullbaiting, and will cite a description by Pepys from the (slightly anachronistic) year 1666.

> After dinner, with my wife and Mercer to the Beare Garden; where I have not been, I think, of many years, and saw some good sport of the bull's tossing the dogs – one into the very boxes. But it is a very rude and nasty pleasure.[34]

We see that the spectacle of a staked bull fighting for his life against packs of attack dogs was family fun, even among gentry, so we may infer that they were not upset by onstage mayhem, whether in *Titus* or in *King Lear,* which is another play impelled by cruelties; without its sublime poetry, *Lear* would be a very rude and nasty pleasure as well.

Once we accept the classification of *Titus Andronicus* as a tragedy of horribilism, we see it for what it is: an immature example of a genre, but a genre that was very popular for all that. It may be helpful to recall a musical analogy that led another great master astray. A modern music-lover may conclude that with *Wellington's Victory* Beethoven laid an egg. But Beethoven was writing in the once-popular genre of the battle-piece, where music is supposed to suggest a military encounter, a genre with a centuries-old pedigree, and to whose

---

[34] Halliday 56.

conventions the composer was scrupulously faithful.   This is not to say that Beethoven did not lay an egg with *Wellington's Victory,* or that Shakespeare did not lay an egg with *Titus Andronicus,* or that there will never be hopeful revivals of either from time to time.   Looking at the tragedy in the proper way, however, will help us to see it for what it is, how to stage it, and how to prepare the audience for it.

A Digression:

Shakespeare in the EFL Classroom

In schools where the students are not native English speakers, there is no pedagogical dividing line between applied English and English literature. Even the most advanced literature students are still busy with mastering the fine points of semantics and style. It is important that literature teachers recognize and respect this continuum. On the other hand, the study of literature can work to the advantage of the EFL teacher, particularly in the case of Shakespeare, from the simple fact of name-recognition. Martin Droeshout's instantly-recognizable engraving of the Bard in the First Folio must be one of the most successful instances of "branding" in history. Shakespeare's particular star-quality, however, is especially strong given the often-encountered opinion outside the Anglosphere that the Bard is not sufficiently appreciated inside the Anglosphere. Werner Habicht has ably chronicled the Germans' long love affair with their "adopted" Shakespeare,[1] which, it will be noted, can be documented to date back to Shakespeare's own lifetime: in 1600 English actors were touring Germany and the Low Countries with a reworked *Titus Andronicus* that is no worse

---

[1] Jansohn 239.

than the Bard's original, and in 1603 with *Der Bestrafte Brudermord* ("the punished fratricide"), a version of *Hamlet* that is so garbled, so unimaginably , unapproachably bad that it must be read to be believed.   Not as well-known, however, is the passion with which Shakespeare has been adopted as the voice of the oppressed in other nations.   Laura Raidonis Bates wrote (in the online journal *Lituanus*) of the Latvian stage that

> Latvian intellectuals - modeling themselves, ironically, on the Russian and German colonizers they were seeking to overthrow - deliberately introduced Shakespeare to the native population as a nationalist tool. Just as in the eighteenth century, Lessing enlisted Shakespeare's aid to oppose foreign French influence on German literature; just as in the mid-nineteenth century, Pushkin enlisted Shakespeare's aid to oppose foreign German influence upon Russian literature; so in the late-nineteenth century, Latvian politico-literary figures...enlisted Shakespeare's aid in opposing *both* German and Russian foreign influence. (Interestingly, in each case, as Shakespeare is used as a model in the formation of an indigenous, national literature, Shakespeare himself is never seen as a "foreign" influence.)[2]

The plays of Shakespeare are not only seen live by theater audiences, but also in movie versions by the larger audiences of motion-picture theaters, television and home video around the world, in English and in other languages as well.   This ubiquity

---

[2]   Raidonis Bates, online

should pique the students' curiosity, and should make the teacher's job that much easier.   Proceeding from glamor to the nuts and bolts of language learning, intermediate-level students can benefit from the study of the many phrases from Shakespeare's plays that are used in everyday English, and that can blend so unobtrusively into grammar exercises that they validate the exercises.   This paper will propose ways to cull these phrases and test them for real-life frequency.   The study of longer passages from Shakespeare's plays offers opportunities to the teacher of advanced EFL.   A play is not a play until it is being performed, and so the advanced student is immediately confronted with issues of pronunciation and extroverted delivery. A selection of speeches and scenes that lend themselves to classroom use will be offered, drawn from the author's teaching experience.

Let it be understood at the outset that I am not proposing this "Shakespearification" as a way to obviate or even to spice up the hard work necessary to acquire the elements of the English language.   On the contrary, I wish to make it clear that my suggestions have no place at all in classes at the beginning levels.   Acquisition of the basics of English grammar and vocabulary must proceed according to the time-honored (and unglamorous) principles of hard work and methodical internalization of language fundamentals.   It makes no sense to introduce "the morn in russet mantle clad" (*Hamlet* 1.1.159) to a beginner: not "morn," because the beginner is still trying to internalize "morning;" not "russet," "mantle" or clad," because that would be asking the student to remember words that he must remember not to use, because they are obsolete or obsolescent.

It is at the intermediate level that Shakespeare can be introduced.   That having been said, it is also important to introduce the Bard in sensible ways and for sensible reasons. As to the reasons, in the context of Chinese students, I preface the issue with a question: why do people say *che shui ma long* ("wagons [like] water [and] horses [like] a dragon") when describing a traffic jam?   The short answer, of course, is because Li Yu said it in a poem; the long answer is that this phrase illustrates the way that a literary quotation can be repeated so often that it is no longer literary: it becomes an anonymous colloquialism.   I remember my grandfather observing from time to time that something was rotten in Denmark, but I never heard him preface his observation by saying "as Shakespeare once said," or by any attribution at all, nor did he ever explain why he said "Denmark" when we were living in west Texas.   The phrase was self-sufficient, and its origin mattered no more than the origin of *che shui ma long*.

It is in this humble, workaday spirit that I propose that Shakespeare be introduced in the intermediate EFL classroom: as a way to improve the student's English.   I will go further and say that this is also the rationale for introducing the Bard in the advanced EFL classroom.   I will go further still and say that this should also be the mindset of the EFL teacher, and the literature teacher, too.

For choosing phrases to introduce in the intermediate-level classroom, it is necessary to avoid the pitfall of including a quotation simply because it has sparkle.   Women with uncommunicative husbands may relish the sting of "Portia is Brutus' harlot, not his wife" (*Julius Caesar* 2.1.287), but only if they and their interlocutors know who Portia is, who Brutus is, and what the problem is.   In the same way that the funniest joke falls flat if it has to be explained, some lines are best left for another day.   There is also the possibility that some of the men in the class may in fact *be* uncommunicative husbands; in this case what is sauce for the goose is not sauce for the gander at all.

The main criterion for introducing a quotation must be whether or not it is usable by a speaker of limited fluency and comprehensible to a hearer of limited vocabulary.   The first question I ask myself is, is it in Bartlett's?   Bartlett's *Familiar Quotations* is a familiar volume in the library of many an English speaker, a sourcebook of quotations from many authors. If a quotation is not in Bartlett's, it is probably not generally known or used.

The second test of frequency is to consult the largest mass of language in the world, the Internet.   This job I leave to the students, who are always poking around the Net anyway.   As a touchstone, in August of 2008, I did a search for "the morn in russet mantle clad."   It yielded a puny nineteen thousand hits, with a high level of redundancy, apparently from nerdy quotation websites; I followed that with a search for "the evil that men do" (*Julius Caesar* 3.2.74), and got an astonishing two hundred and forty-one *million* hits from a variety of websites, including music and cinema as well as drama.

My final test is a negative one: I glance at the EFL material the students are using, to make sure that the quotation is not off the mark.   If the class is studying superlatives, "the most unkindest cut of all" (*Julius Caesar* 3.2.180) is a bad choice, because it undercuts what the students are learning.   The same is true for "No, nor woman, neither" (*Hamlet* 2.2.312) if the subject is negatives.

The first Bartlett's quotation that meets these criteria is "What's mine is yours, and what is yours is mine" (*Measure for Measure* 5.1.534). Well, that's certainly non-threatening. It also has an attractive touch of unexpected content. In the same spirit, when the student is practicing phrases involving "too much of" something, why not slip in "too much of a good thing" (*As You Like It* 1.4.120)? There is, after all, not much room for creativity when speaking of "too much salt," but the quotation, leading as it does to the idea of "too much money," or "too much time on his hands," is a springboard for all kinds of speculative discussion.

In midst of a lesson involving "have eaten, "have written," have-this, have-that, when the class is dealing with "I have seen...," I recommend another Shakespeare phrase that has entered everyday English, "We have seen better days" (*As You Like It* 2.7.120). If the phrase is sometimes heard from native speakers as "Uncle Fred has seen..." or "my overcoat has seen...," then so much the better. This kind of real-life validation of classroom exercises, this glimpse down the road, as it were, gives the student the assurance that his time is being well spent. When the subject is time expressions, and "forever" comes up, it is apropos to introduce "For ever and a day" (*As You Like It* 4.1.142). With compounds in –*able*, it is interesting to note that "answerable," "unmatchable" and "laughable" are evidently Shakespearean coinages.[3]

For advanced classes, the unit of instruction is no longer the word or the line, but the passage, perhaps even the scene. The scene that I have found to be the most successful, both in terms

---

[3]　Potter 47.

of objectively-measured results like the introduction of well-known phrases and in subjectively-measured ones like student enthusiasm, is *Julius Caesar* Act III, scene 2, the "Brutus is an honorable man" scene, the same "the evil that men do" scene that I have already alluded to.   Brutus' appeal to the head (and the naiveté of it), Antony's appeal to the heart (and the brazenness of it) and the fickleness of the mob, never fail to elicit my students' commentary and questions.   I have the students read the passage aloud, each student reading from four to ten lines at a time.   The first reading is a very picky micro-reading, to make sure that the students understand the language elements of vocabulary and intangibles like quotability. The second reading is a theatrical reading focusing on the content, but not forgetting pronunciation.   I have found that three two-hour sessions are sufficient for this treatment.

A more ambitious reading, requiring at least four two-hour sessions, is the "casket" scenes from *The Merchant of Venice*. It is important for the student to understand the effect of the double plot, so I "bracket" the Portia material with the business of Antonio's debt.   For this reason I begin by assigning Act I, scene 3, where Shylock drives his hard bargain; then we go on to the box scenes themselves.

A note on methodology is in order about the first of these. The message that Morocco finds in the box that he chooses (*The Merchant of Venice* 2.7.65) contains another phrase that should elicit creative oral and written response, although not as effortlessly introduced, since it involves a low-frequency word. This is the idea that "All that glitters is not gold."   Never mind that the original has "glisters;" every native speaker I've ever heard quote it has said "glitters," so "glitters" it shall be in the EFL classroom.

The "silver" scene (2.9) requires no commentary, but there are two points that need to be made about the "lead" scene. First, there is the matter of the song that is sung while Bassanio makes up his mind.   I blush to admit it, but for forty-odd years of reading Shakespeare, I never gave its lyrics a second thought. It was not until July of 2008 that Horst Meller, in his essay "Mark the Music," enlightened me.

> Portia is not supposed to prompt.   But from fairy tales one knows that sometimes secret messages may be sung although they must not be told.   And so the riddle *Tell me where is Fancy bred* is sung to music while Bassanio ponders and comments on the caskets himself.   He may well take the clue: three out of eight lines in the charming song rhyme with *lead*:   bred, head, nourishèd.[4]

I intend to propose Meller's insight to my students in the form of a riddle ("How is Portia helping?").   If it takes them forty-odd years to solve it, that will be time well spent.

There is another detail about the "lead" scene (3.2) that is helpful: it ends with a transition back to the business of Antonio's debt, which rounds the readings out nicely.   Thus the assignment for this last scene is 3.2.1-149, then line 220 to the end.

It may be that there are advantages to working the scenes up to the performance level, by which I mean memorized speeches

---

[4]   Jansohn 199.

and stage movement, perhaps even costumes, but I prefer not to go beyond classroom reading.   There is a vanishing point to any endeavor, and rather than hammering away at one scene, I believe that class time is better spent introducing a variety of scenes with different moods.   There is also a matter of personal taste: I got to know Shakespeare in high school by reading plays in literature classes (*The Taming of the Shrew* and *Hamlet*), and by seeing them in college productions (*Richard III* and *The Tempest* at nearby Texas Tech University), but the medium which I enjoyed the most was the spoken word sound recording. My little hometown library had recordings of abridged versions of the plays, with actors from the Old Vic, if I remember correctly; I thought of Sean Connery as Hotspur long after everyone else thought of him as Agent 007.   Audio, "the theater of the mind," has been my preferred medium for Shakespeare ever since, immune as it is from the excesses of self-indulgent actors and self-important directors.   As a teacher I have always rejected attempts to use visual media to teach auditory skills like pronunciation and comprehension, and so I have my students at Chinese Culture University, who as non-native speakers of English are both literature students and EFL students, confine their in-class performances to the spoken word, sitting at their desks and relying on their voices alone.

Excerpts from Shakespeare are not the main course in an EFL classroom, but as a garnish they can provide the variety of unexpected content and a hint of rewards to come.

De Facto Anonymity:

Grimm's Fairy Tales

Everyone has his favorite *Grimm's Fairy Tales* characters. Mine are the old soldier and the flea-market lady. Should the reader find himself at a loss to recall the tales in which these two appear, this is natural, since they are not characters in the *Tales* at all, but real-life, flesh-and-blood storytellers whose tales were recorded by Jacob and Wilhelm Grimm.

Neither itinerant market worker Dorothea Viehmann (1755-1815) nor Sergeant of Dragoons Johann Friedrich Krause (1747-1828) would have left any footprints in the sands of time whatever had they never met the Brothers Grimm, who gave them a place in German literature by including their stories in *KHM* (the usual abbreviation of the collection, from the German *Kinder- und Hausmärchen*, "children's and house tales"), or rather — given the popularity of the *Tales* — gave them a place in world literature. Viehmann was the most prolific single source of material for *KHM* (credited with no fewer than twenty-eight stories in Hans-Jörg Uther's meticulous edition, with §22 marked as questionable). Krause told the sort of tales that were to be expected of a penniless old man who had outlived his usefulness to the Hessian army (rather like the old dog in §48,

Der alte Sultan ["old Sultan"]), yarns of penury and rootlessness on one hand, and on the other, fantasies of wealth and standing.

There is an important sense, however, in which the old soldier and the flea-market lady return the Grimms' favor by giving us a behind-the-scenes glimpse of the Brothers at work. For the majority of readers, the stories in *KHM* are accepted, to use a modern-day flea-market term, "as is, where is," without any interest in their origins, context or purpose. "As is, where is" is, in fact, appropriate for the majority of the *Tales*: they seem to belong to a dream world, out of space and time, as orderly as a string of pearls. We need not look far for evidence that the Brothers Grimm were editors as well as collectors: the simple fact that the majority of the *Tales* are in good, mellifluous, standard German should tell us that there was some editorial smoothing-out on the part of the Grimms. Six *Tales*, in fact, are recorded "raw," that is, in the local German dialect (to all intents and purposes unintelligible), and Grimm specialist Heinz Rölleke analyzes sixteen stories exhaustively, with helpful notes on dialect words, literary antecedents and anthropological notes,[1] which provides us with a touchstone as to how the others were edited for literary style. Rölleke elsewhere provides a comprehensive overview of the state of the question, including the genesis of the collection, the question of the antiquity of the tales, literary antecedents, and a breakdown of sources: no fewer than sixteen are literary.[2]

---

[1]   Rölleke1998, *passim.*
[2]   Rölleke1985, 74.

We may take it as a given that the majority of the *Tales* are in standard German as a result of the editors' hand. But how heavy was that hand?

At times it was not heavy at all. In story §36* (*Tischchen deck dich, Goldesel und Knüppel aus dem Sack,* "table be set, gold-donkey and stick from the sack"), we find duly recorded Krause's folksy aside,

> *Ich sehe dir's an, du wärst auch gerne dabeigewesen.*
> ("I can tell by looking at you that you would have liked to have been there.")

In my mind's eye I see Krause leaning over the table, winking conspiratorially at Wilhelm Grimm, who dutifully copies even as he shudders. *Du* in German, after all, is not the way one addresses college professors. He must also have shuddered at the story itself, where gold "spews" from a donkey; and here I suspect the editor's intervention in the interests of propriety. The German word for "spew" is *speien,* which is normally used of oral discharges like spitting and vomiting. But donkeys are not noted for salivation; Grimm wrote that the emission came _hintern_ *und vorn* ("front and <u>back</u>"); I take the *vorn,* and for that matter, the *speien,* to be a bowdlerization of a soldierly vulgarism: I don't know about the Hessian army, but in the American one, when payday is referred to as "when the Eagle screams," "screams" is a euphemism.

---

* This tale is not ordinarily attributed to Krause; my reasons for doing so will be seen on p. 177.

We must look not only at the Grimms, however, but at ourselves. We see what we are prepared to see. "Old soldier" and "flea-market lady" meant very different things to *KHM*'s first readers than to us, as can be seen when we examine evidence from and about the world in which *KHM* appeared.

The last of the sixty-four very weighty volumes of Johann Heinrich Zedler's *Grosses vollständiges Universal-Lexicon* ("Great Complete Universal Lexicon") was published in 1750. This was before Dorothea Viehmann was born, true, but only five years before; the anachronism is slight, and the insights are great if we use this work as a time capsule, opening it to the article on Viehmann's homeland, the old German kingdom of Hesse.

Zedler's article would suggest that Viehmann's girlhood was spent in bucolic surroundings, where people had little else to do but idle around and tell stories to kill time. After a catalogue of classical references to the area,[3] a leisurely genealogy of the ruling class[4] and the identification of the country as Lutheran[5], the author informs us that the land is rich, that it produces fine silver, a lot of iron and steel, a good wine (an export item), and even tobacco.[6]

A closer look, however, dispels any mental picture the reader may have of merry peasants polka-ing in front of thatch-roofed cottages. Far from being idyllic, Hesse was a brutal, rapacious tyranny whose main export was cannon fodder. American history notes Hessians briefly, as soldiers employed in

---

[3] Zedler 1899.
[4] Zedler 1900-1901.
[5] Zedler 1901.
[6] Zedler 1901-02.

the Revolutionary War by the Crown (one of whom would be the ancestor of George Armstrong Custer); Hesse as a mercenary state had already had a long history, however, and would continue to supply men for cash up to the end of the Napoleonic era, 1815, which, by an interesting coincidence, was the year Dorothea Viehmann died. Her birth year, as mentioned above, was the beginning of hostilities in the Seven Years War; and she was a young woman when thousands of Hesse's young men marched off to fight in the American Colonies.

Before discussing the societal impact of these three wars (the Seven Years War, the American Revolution, and the wars with the French), we need to take a harder look at the sort of life the Hessians led. An examination by Peter Taylor of historical documents concerning the western part of Hesse reveals a grimmer picture than that recounted by Zedler.

> Since the Thirty Years War, the region of Oberhessen has impressed most observers with its poverty. This area of 1100 square kilometers...did not become a food-exporting region until near the end of the eighteenth century and only during times of dearth elsewhere. In 1782, most of its nearly 50,000 inhabitants wrested a meager existence out of the rough, stony soils of this heavily forested region.[7]

Although Taylor does not mention tobacco, he finds that the agriculture of the region was actually more varied than Zedler recounts.

---

[7] Taylor 115-6.

> Rural economic enterprise took varied forms of mixed livestock and grain farming supplemented by rural industry...Peasants grew, in order of abundance, rye..., barley..., oats..., and wheat... In addition to working cropland..., peasants also grew hay...on meadows..., and cabbages..., beets...and other greens in smaller garden plots.[8]

Produce prices would rise in response to crop failures in other parts of Germany, and a graph on p. 117 of Taylor's book records an astonishing "spike" during the Seven Years War. The small farmers benefited little from this, however.

> With price trends generally upward, peasant producers might have gotten more wealthy but there is little evidence that they did so—a fact probably explained by the increasingly extractive state... Moreover, peasants probably did not market the bulk of their own grain crops. Rather, tributary overlords who collected tithes and ground-rents in kind brought a large portion of the grain to market... Much of the harvest remained at home in household and village economies still dominated by subsistence imperatives...The slow rate of agricultural intensification suggests the inflexibility of the agricultural tribute-taking system, militarily-caused labor shortages, and an endemic shortage of investment capital.[9]

---

[8] Taylor 116-118.
[9] Taylor 119-120.

On the farm, perhaps, but we will shortly see that the cities, including Kassel, were awash in capital.

> Those peasants who had goods to sell had places to sell them.
> [Frankfurt and Marburg] provided the largest regional markets while peasants also used village markets at Ebsdorf, Lohra, and Fronhausen.   The latter two played some role for the peasants of Oberweimar even though Marburg was as close.   Commodities found in city and village trading centers included grain, livestock, pottery, linen and wool in various stages of completion, and leather. Rural dwellers often produced manufactured goods in certain villages which specialized in pottery or leather or other particular products.   Jews provided a network of trans-local and itinerant livestock traders that tied the region to producers and consumers on the outside. Parishes such as Oberweimar might have one or two resident Jewish households that traded in cattle and processed meat as well as linking the parish to wider markets.[10]

Here we pause; the German word for "livestock" is *Vieh.* Dorothea Viehmann is spoken of as an itinerant market worker. Could *Viehmann* be an occupational name?   It is certainly an unusual name.   It is known that she was of French Huguenot ancestry; could Dorothea Viehmann have been Jewish by marriage?

---

[10] Taylor 120.

Returning to our overview of Hesse, it is time to detail the shadow cast over the landscape: *Soldatenhandel,* a term difficult to render without losing its dreadful casualness.   On the analogy of the slangy *showbiz,* I opt for *soldierbiz,* to reflect the offhandedness with which the mercenary nature of the Hessian military was viewed, taken for granted as it had been for a century. Charles Ingrao's study of contemporary records provides a great deal of information to flesh out our mental picture of J.F. Krause.

> Ultimately, the needs and desires of the very few buyers (mostly England France, and the Netherlands) who entered the international soldier trade determined the standards in the internal soldier trade and on the drill ground.   The Landgraves of Hesse-Cassel depended on the subsidies acquired thorough this commerce.   Thus, as tiny parts of a very well-oiled machine, the soldiers of Hesse-Cassel were essential to the financial integrity of the Landgrave and the Hessian state, and were engaged in virtually every major European conflict of arms during the eighteenth century. It was rare that these soldiers played the role of defender of the hearth and home to which we, in our more nationalistic times have become accustomed.   More often, they defended the interests of other princes in other lands and toward the end of the century gained a reputation as one of Europe's finest armies.[11]

In a nutshell, the king, in this case Frederick II, would contract with a foreign power to provide a certain number of troops, and

---

[11] Ingrao 211.

his recruiters would get busy, coaxing, bamboozling and kidnapping until they had enlisted enough men to meet their quota. Lest we be too hard on the recruiters, let us remember that His Majesty was a cad as well. In the case of the American Revolution royal duplicity may explain why Viehmann usually portrays kings as scoundrels.

> Having already negotiated and advertised British pay scales for its soldiers, [Frederick] decided...to reduce the five-taler monthly wage by half, with the intention of pocketing the rest.[12]

There was an outcry, and a near mutiny. His Highness backed down.

> The British ultimately compelled Frederick to restore the full five-taler wage.[13]

This example of forced honesty was the exception, not the rule. We read of

> ...poorer and less skilled solders who had originally joined the militia thinking it entailed only three weeks of local service but who now did not want to leave their families to accompany the regular army to America... In desperation some families actually hid their sons shortly before departure or encouraged them to desert. In one tragic case

---

[12] Ingrao 141.
[13] Ingrao 142.

an elderly widower even cut off one of his son's fingers in order to secure his release.   Instead he and his son were jailed, and a few days later he committed suicide.[14]

If evasion of conscription was punished, the Hessian government was at its harshest on the question of desertion.

> After a soldier had been declared a deserter the military not only seized his disposable wealth but also inventoried his parents' property in order to calculate his portion of the family inheritance, which was then seized on their death. Once the military had confiscated and resold this property, it carefully recorded the proceeds of each transaction...The poverty of Hessian deserters assumes an even more dramatic profile when we account for those hundreds of native deserters whose names never appear in the military's record of confiscations because they were likely either completely penniless or had no realistic prospects of inheriting a share of their parents' wealth – such as younger sons... or youths whose parents were still years way from death.[15]
>
> The cumulative picture is one of a Hessian soldiery that was almost uniformly destitute, comprising as it did both disinherited younger sons and elder brothers who were hardly any better off...   Neither the Hessian Landgraves nor their Prussian successors ever allowed Hessian youths many alternatives to being soldiers.[16]

---

[14] Ingrao 142.
[15] Ingrao 161-2.
[16] Ingrao 190-1.

The American venture, however, was not popular, and to fill their quotas

> ...by 1779, desperate Hessian recruiters were regularly abducting foreign subjects traveling through Hesse-Cassel, as well as some living just across the frontier.[17]

Despite the widespread hardship and fear that the mercenary state's voracity caused throughout the countryside, the new manufacturing businesses in Hessian towns benefited: vast amounts of soldierbiz hard currency flowed into the royal coffers, and this led to a boom for those shrewd enough to profit from the dislocations in the economy.

> Hesse-Cassel's commercial economy also benefited as expected. The army's ongoing need for weaponry and munitions returned Schmalkalden's iron industry to profitability after a frustrating decade-long search for new markets. Since the entire army needed new uniforms virtually every year of the war, the country's textile industry was also able to increase production by about 20 percent...

(The new uniforms, it must be noted, were replaced at the soldier's expense, not the government's. This recalls the U.S. Army marching song, "They say that in the Army / The pay is mighty fine. / They give you a hundred dollars / And take back ninety-nine.")

---

[17] Ingrao 144.

As might be expected, these positive commercial developments had their greatest impact in the towns, which now interrupted their long-term demographic stagnation with population gains that averaged 4.2 percent during the period 1773-81.[18]

In the countryside, however, the quest was not for economic opportunities, but for survival of self and loved ones from the man-devouring military machine. Families took advantage of every loophole they could, even at the expense of drastic reorganization of assets.

If middling farmers...divided their estates to settle and exempt as many of their sons as possible, this meant sacrifices undoubtedly had to be made in their daughters' marriage portions. Such reductions made them less attractive matches for the sons of the wealthy. Concomitantly, as the capacity to attract wealthy males diminished, the need increased for poor brides to marry the growing number of poor men who were being settled to avoid the draft. More and more frequently, then, did marriage partners come from the same classes of wealth. The new pattern reduced the number of social ties across the chasms of wealth which were increasingly separating villagers from one another.[19]

Many families, however, were too poor for ruses like these, and so resisted on a lower level.

---

[18] Ingrao 146.
[19] Ingrao 184.

There was no widespread peasant violence, and so we must look instead for subtler forms of erosion... The most obvious disorders came in the form of large-scale emigration by draft-eligible males. Beyond even these desperate acts, Landräte [local councils] reported the flight of whole families and village populations on the approach of recruitment officials.[20]

The anguish caused by the soldiers' departure led to societal strain and occasional breakdown; later, Hesse would have to deal with the anguish caused by the soldiers' return.

As early as 1763, one official from Wanfried accused released veterans of dishonoring village girls, setting up illegal households with them on common land, illegally using common grazing areas for their livestock, and finally terrorizing village officials to prevent their behavior from being reported.[21]

The most obvious case of breakdown in the processes of patrimonial [i.e. government-delegated] authority came when the Landgrave ordered that villagers accept the returning veterans of the American campaign with open arms. Villagers, remembering the bad experiences with veterans of the Seven Years War, simply refused to allow veterans to establish themselves.[22]

Here the axes were meaningless petty rules enforced by torture and an underworld morality in which the soldier was

---

[20] Ingrao 192.
[21] Ingrao 187.
[22] Ingrao 193.

stripped of any sense of accountability to anything but survival and stolen pleasures. The psychological resolution of these contradictions between one social arena and the other can hardly have been an easy task.[23]

The demoralizing nature of barracks life and military training, combined with the legal and financial incapacity to form everyday social relationships, transmuted soldiers into sources of sexual danger and familial chaos in the eyes of people who lived with them.[24]

Lived in the same house with them, that is.

Those who negotiated marriage contracts in the 1780's frequently wrote into those contracts that veteran siblings of the couple "shall receive free room and board in the house for the rest of" their lives.[25]

The intrusion of hardened infantrymen into civilian life at such close quarters was explosive, and a pervasive distortion of the social order.

Officials expressed growing concern for the erosion of parental authority. They referred particularly to parents who had given up farms to their children early and had subsequently experienced beatings and verbal abuse from their heirs. Authorities warned that such children were not only "offenders against nature, but transgressed against God's law and worldly legislation."[26]

---

[23] Ingrao 210.
[24] Ingrao 222.
[25] Ingrao 215.
[26] Ingrao 176-7.

Soldiers also opened the door to family chaos: "as we have seen, resources were diverted to the care of veterans, violent persons were introduced into family settings, labor routines were disorganized, and conflicts over inheritance arose."[27]

Even when court sessions did proceed, they were punctuated by violence and rough language more often than in the past, further suggesting a growing tension and lack of order... Although the records of fines do not permit a direct connection between the tyranny of conscription and this breakdown of authority, village headmen and other officials did blame the draft and its consequences for their own growing unwillingness to serve the Landrat further.[28]

Ingrao goes on to apply this Big Picture to Grimm's *KHM*, but his ideas are beyond the scope of this paper; besides, the treatment in his book is only a paraphrase of a paper he co-authored with Hermann Rebel in *Journal of Family History,* which is the form in which his thesis should be addressed. The present work, however, does have one memorable *bon mot* on the question of the worth of *KHM* as ethnography, of throwing out the baby with the bathwater.

> Coming at a time when historians and ethnographers have begun using such materials to try to give poor people a voice in historical accounts, the attack on the integrity of the Grimms as collectors of tales threatens permanent laryngitis to the unheard.[29]

---

[27] Ingrao 223.

[28] Ingrao 193.

[29] Ingrao 232.

Dorothea Viehmann and J.F. Krause were not unheard, thanks to the Brothers Grimm.   Yet understanding the cultural context in which all four lived, along with the other tale tellers, helps us, paradoxically, to hear the silence they record: a bare mention of a discharged soldier, for example, cannot begin to convey to us moderns the fear and disgust that the *Tales'* original audience felt; Viehmann, more than the others, breaks the silence for those who have ears to hear: her lying kings, her *Frieder* tale (when "Freddy" would have instantly reminded the audience that the reigning monarch was Frederick II) , her crafty servants and between-the-lines commentary, all take the tales up to the limit of the permissible.

Given the force of personality that her tales reveal, it seems odd that Viehmann has never been treated as an author in her own right.   What the Grimms produced, after all, is an *edited anthology*; *KHM* is plural, not singular.   The originality and artistry of Viehmann's stories should also have earned her her own niche in German literature (although perhaps not in world literature).   The reader of §61, *Das Bürle* ("The Li'l Farmer"), with its theme of desperate, unseemly craving for cow-ownership, is instantly reminded of Scene 11 of Brecht's *Mutter Courage,* where the peasant family defiantly refuses to betray their side to the enemy (*Ich dien nicht die Katholischen...Ich tus nicht ums Leben:*   "I don't serve the Catholics...I'd rather die.") – until their two cows and one ox are threatened.   One soldier says,

...Hör zu: wenn du keine Vernunft annimmst, säbel ich das Vieh nieder.
DER JUNGE BAUER   Nicht das Vieh!

DIE BÄUERIN Herr Hauptmann, verschont unser Vieh, wir möchten's sonst verhungern!...

DER JUNGE BAUER Zum Alten *Muß ich's tun?* Die Bäuerin nickt. *Ich tus.*

("...Listen: if you don't listen to reason, I'll "saber" the livestock down.

THE YOUNG PEASANT Not the livestock!

THE PEASANT'S WIFE Captain, spare our livestock! We'd starve otherwise!...

THE YOUNG PEASANT *To the old one* Must I do it? *The wife nods.* I'll do it.")

What is sauce for Brecht's goose should be sauce for Viehmann's gander. I do not say that the *Märchenfrau* should be considered a German Master, as Brecht certainly was (this vignette, after all, is only the set-up for the thrilling, almost unwatchable climax of *Mutter Courage*), but I do say that she deserves author status — perhaps an anthology of her own.

Setting aside the question of topic, Viehmann's diction is of enormous interest, having proto-Brechtian characteristics: she uses clichés out of context, Bible passages out of context (although without Brecht's sarcasm), blandly juxtaposes outrageously disparate images, displays a flair for *le mot juste,* and is a superb exemplar of peasant wiliness and have-not hatred of the haves (§58, *Der Hund und der Sperling,* "The Dog and the Sparrow," is a particularly forceful portrayal of revenge of the weak against the strong).

One also notes that in addition to these proto-Brechtian traits, she also demonstrates proto-Wodehousian ones in the way her omniscient servants steer their empty-headed masters clear of trouble (§6, *Der treue Johannes,* "Faithful John," and §57,

Der goldene Vogel, "The Golden Bird," where Faithful John is reincarnated as an omniscient and unfailingly patient fox); this has to do with plot, though, not with the parameters mentioned above, and it is Viehmann's verbal originality that is most striking.

Viehmann's wordplay is not just a string of one-liners; she is artful with the foreground of her creations, but equally elegant with their background, the set-ups of the high points of the stories.   Also of note is the decisiveness with which she veers between high and low, juxtaposing moments of high intensity with the most tepid clichés imaginable. An example from §29, *Der Teufel mit den drei goldenen Haaren,* ("The Devil with the Three Golden Hairs"):   in suspense and dread the hero travels to the Devil's own home over gnarled trees and crags, only to find the cozy sort of dwelling that the Germans call Biedermeier ("comfortable, conventional, respectable, bougeois"), where Beelzebub's *Ellermutter* ("Granny") is sitting in a *Sorgenstuhl* ("easy chair;" in §22, *Das Rätsel* ["The Riddle"] the witch is in a *Lehnstuhl* ["armchair"]).   Like a good middle-class wage-earner, Lucifer comes home at dusk (we infer, directly from "work"), but launches into a tirade because the house isn't tidy enough, and starts rummaging around, having smelled the hero's "human flesh."   A Biedermeier devil!   The sauciness of Granny's reply suggests that Frau Viehmann worked as a domestic at one point, and though she may have bitten her tongue then, she gives Granny an acrid reply:

Eben ist erst gekehrt...und alles in Ordnung gebracht, nun wirfst du mir's wieder untereinander; immer hast du Menschenfleisch in der Nase!   Setze dich und iß dein Abendbrot.

("It's just been swept...and everything straightened up. Now you're turning everything upside-down. You've always got human flesh in your nose! Sit down and eat your supper.")

The Devil, subdued, does so. The tables are turned, however, when Granny, to help the hero, pulls out one of the Devil's hairs while he sleeps. What do you say to His Satanic Majesty when he's in a rage? It would be hard to imagine a blander, more anticlimactic reply than her

Nimm's nicht übel.

("Don't be offended.")

The irritated Devil threatens her, not with fire and brimstone, but by saying

...wenn du mich noch einmal im Schlafe stört, so kriegst du eine Ohrfeige.
("...if you disturb me while I sleep one more time, you'll get a slap on the head.")

The above effort notwithstanding, it is with §125, *Der Teufel und seine Großmutter* ("The Devil and his Grandmother") where Viehmann outdoes herself with her Biedermeier-Satan effort. Grandma fixes a nice supper for the Old Dragon.

Da fragte sie ihn im Gespräch, wie's den Tag ergangen wäre und wieviel Seelen er kriegt hätte. »Es wollte mir heute nicht recht glücken,« antwortete er...

("Then she asked him in conversation how the day had gone, and how many souls he'd gotten hold of. 'I didn't have much luck today,' he answered...").

At times the incongruous diction does not elicit a chuckle, but a belly-laugh, as in §31, *Das Mädchen ohne Hände* ("the girl without hands"), when the girl's response to her father's intention to cut her hands off is the preposterously bland, *Lieber Vater, macht mit mir, was Ihr wollt, ich bin Euer Kind* ("dear Father, do with me as you will; I am your child"). In my mind's eye I see Viehmann, the salty, tough old flea-market survivor, going deadpan and adopting an *ingenue* tone as she delivered the line.   This sort of panache reveals the "pro."

Viehmann is also a "pro," in the sense that she had a definite way of doing things.   Turns of phrase occur again and again.   In §106, Der *arme Müllerbursch und das Kätzchen* ("The Poor Miller-Boy and the Kitty") for example, a benefactor's offered aid is rejected with the following formula: *Ach, du kannst mir doch nicht helfen.* ("Oh, you can't help me.") In §125 a similar offer elicits, *Ach, was liegt Euch daran, Ihr könnt uns doch nicht helfen.* ("Oh, what's it to you?   You can't help us.")   There is a variant in §29, where Granny says   *...ich will sehen, ob ich dir helfen kann.*   ("...I'll see if I can help you.")

§34 has Intelligent Elsie dithering about what to do first:

Was tu ich?   Schneid ich eh'r, oder eß ich eh'r?   Hei, ich will erst essen...Was tu ich?   Schneid ich eh'r oder schlaf ich eh'r? Hei, ich will erst schlafen.

("What do I do, cut [wheat] first, or eat first?   Oh, I want
to eat first...What do I do?   Cut first or sleep first?   Oh, I
want to sleep first.")

§59, *Der Frieder und das Catherlieschen* ("Freddy and
Cathylee") has Catherlieschen asking herself

Eß ich, eh ich schneid, oder schlaf ich, eh ich schneid?
Hei, ich will eh'r essen!
("Do I eat before I cut, or sleep before I cut?   Oh, I want
to eat first!")

but she falls asleep afterward.   Both stories also share a *shtick*
where the heroine, unsure if she exists, knocks on her own door
to see if she is home.

Other details are constant: service is regularly for seven
years (§31, §100, §106); the Devil is regularly a dragon (§29,
§100, §125); sweeping recurs often enough to reinforce the idea
that Viehmann may at some point have worked as a maid.

Her word for "sweepings" *Kehrdreck* ("sweep-crap") is not
in the dictionary, but should be.   This brings up the subject of
Viehmann's vivid turns of phrase.   In §125 we read of a
steinalte Frau ("stone-old woman," equivalent to "old as the
hills"); there is the low-frequency word *bäumeln* ("dangle," as
from a gallows); in the same story there is *Geld wie Heu*
("money like hay"), and its echo in §61, *wo der goldene Schnee*
fällt, "where the golden snow falls"); in §34, *Die kluge Else*,
("Intelligent Elsie") there is quite a feast: *...und als sie dick*
satt war ("and when she was fat-satisfied"); *Sie hat Zwirn im*
Kopf ("She has twine in her head," meaning "She's a sharp

cookie"), *die...hört die Fliegen husten* ("She hears the flies clear their throats," meaning "She doesn't miss a trick"); and the charming closing tag, *Mein Märchen ist aus, dort lauft eine Maus* ("my story is done, see the little mouse run.")   .

On the other hand, there are times when a Viehmann phrase seems curiously flat, imprecise. §125 has the nobility *in Wagen führen* ("riding in wagons"), although in a later reference she has them in carriages; §106 has *kleinmachen* ("make small"), a very imprecise way of saying *chop* firewood; and in §29 an even more imprecise phrase, *zu einem tiefen Wasser kam* ("came to a deep water").

At other times Viehmann adopts the grand, sententious style.   Cinderella's lazy sisters (§21) unctuously intone *Wer Brot essen will, soll es verdienen* ("He who would eat bread, must earn it"); in §71, *Sechse kommen durch die ganze Welt* ("Six Against the World"), the princess gloats *Der Feind ist in meine Hände gegeben* ("The foe is given into my hands"); and there is the solemn *so sterb ich getrost und in Frieden* ("thus I die comforted and in peace").   And how Wilhelm Grimm's pen must have recoiled from the loan-word *pures Gold* ("pure gold"), instead of the purer *reines*!

This survey of Dorothea Viehmann's style is by no means exhaustive, and does not even attempt to answer a very important question: Why, after their initial enthusiasm for Viehmann's stories, did the Brothers Grimm drop references to her in later editions?   What had changed?

(Duly set off in parentheses, my own theory is that the reason Viehmann was "dumped" was the same as the reason she had been previously embraced; put more exactly, we are speaking of two sides of the same coin.   The Grimms began their folklore research with the assumption that folk tales are like time capsules that preserve the past for the present. Their efforts, however, resulted in not one work, but two, *KHM* and a parallel masterpiece, *Deutsche Sagen* ["German legends"]. *Deutsche Sagen* holds true to the "time capsule" thesis. I take it that, in the Brothers' minds, *KHM* did not. They probably started with that assumption: earlier I have pictured the Grimms earnestly scribbling every word that the garrulous veteran J. F. Krause uttered; yet observers as intelligent as the Grimms must have realized in time that Krause's gratuitous editorializing was not part of the age-old narrative, and they must have generalized their conclusions to their other informants, named and unnamed. Finally they applied their conclusions to themselves: if Viehmann can tailor a tale to a particular audience, why can't we? After all, they had familiarized themselves with the idiom, mastered it, stripped away its mystique: they had become storytellers themselves, and were just as entitled to adapt the tales as any of their informants. Here endeth the guesswork.)

The cold, hard fact is that we will never know why Dorothea Viehmann became a non-person: Jacob and Wilhelm Grimm are unavailable for comment, and even if a hand-written explanation were to be discovered tomorrow, I would not trust it. The Grimms were great scholars, but they were not saints, as we shall see when we examine the old soldier's tales.

Krause's palette is not as extroverted as Viehmann's, but is still noteworthy for its military "accent." In two stories that were included in the Grimm's first edition (but omitted thereafter), *Herr Fix-und-Fertig* ("Mister Rid-and-Ready," since the Grimms observe[30] that *In Pommern heißt Meister Fiks der Scharfrichter* ["that in Pomeramia '*Master Fiks*' is the term for the executioner"]) and *Von der Serviette, dem Tornister, dem Kanonenhütlein und dem Horn* ("about the napkin, the knapsack, the little canon-hat and the horn") are soldier's tales; and there are details of the stories that are instructive, particularly because the second of these two stories   appears to have been reworked into §36, as mentioned above (which is why I have attributed the tale to Krause, as above, p. 157).   If this is true, it is an example of the Grimms' editorial hand being much heavier than in the donkey episode referred to in that tale.   In §36, the hero climbs a tree and sees *die Gipfel der Bäume* ("the crest of the trees," as if the forest were an undifferentiated mass), whereas Krause had *die Spitze der Bäume* ("the points of the trees," as if they were massed bayonets); one imagines Jacob's pen recoiling from the loan-word *Serviette* ("napkin"), and the relief he felt at changing it (§36) to the purer *Tüchlein*; and in "Sultan" (another loan-word; momentarily focusing on Krause rather than Grimm, one notes that foreign words are a constant in soldierly language) the cat's tail is mistaken, not for a garden-variety *Schwert* ("sword"), but for the very precise *Säbel* ("saber"), which may in turn have been subconsciously suggested by the cat's weird gait, since *Säbelbeinig* (literally "saber-legged") means "bandy-legged."

Krause's contribution to the tales was the point of departure for a proposed rethinking of *KHM* by Gonthier-Louis Fink in 1993.   Fink begins by posing the question of whether fairy tales are escapist or are in fact thinly-disguised allegories of everyday

---

[30] Bolte & Polívka, 2:19

life.   Normally this would be an idle question, since some stories are clearly aimed at this or that personage, institution or class, as in Aesop's fables, where predatory animals (lions and wolves) behave unmistakably like predatory people (bosses or officials), but some stories have no evident target, and seem vague by nature.   Fink makes his inquiry pointed, however, by asking it specifically of the Brothers Grimm, and linking it to the class origins of their informants.   He stresses the middle-class origins of the Grimms' informants, and the fact that 80-90% of them were women.   Only a few informants "belonged to the folk".   Surprisingly, Dorothea Viehmann is excluded, having an allegedly French outlook.

This has nothing to do with the Grimms' explicit distinction between *Volkspoesie* (broadly cultural) and *Kunstpoesie* (specifically individual), the first assumed to emmanate from the culture, the other being individual, and possibly contrived.   Instead, one senses the "B" word, *Biedermeier*, but used by Fink not in the entertaining, creative sense we have observed in the work of Viehmann, but in the resentful sense of reverse snobbery toward German middle-class propriety — and inhibitions — that are incompatible with the romantic, free-spirited, glamorous lives of German scribblers. Fink has no monopoly on this: as early as in the theater-preface to *Faust,* Goethe's poet reacts to the suggestion that he write something that will entertain the audience, thus:

> *Ihr fühlet nicht, wie schlecht ein solches Handwerk sei!*
> *Wie wenig das dem echten Künstler zieme!* 105.
> *Der saubern Herren Pfuscherei*
> *Ist, merk' ich, schon bei Euch Maxime.*

("You do not feel what drudgery that would be!
How unseemly for the pure artist!
Slapdashery for the neat gentlemen
Is, I note, a rule of thumb for you.")

Fink's contrast between folk and non-folk implies a contrast between stories that are prettified, euphemized and, to use Goethe's slur, *neat*, on one hand, and gritty, plain-spoken and Gorky-esque on the other.

Whatever the merits of this outlook in the abstract, it is clearly out of place when applied specifically to *KHM*, as we sense from an important nuance on the title page of the Grimms' first edition: the stories are said to be *gesammelt* ("collected") *durch* Jacob and Wilhelm: the authorial *von* ("by") is not used, but *durch*, "through," as if the brothers were merely the passive channel through which the stories passed.   This is disingenuous: comparison of earlier and later versions of the tales reveal that a great deal of revising went on, that the stories went *through* a maze of changes, and many of the changes would qualify as Biedermeierisms.   Schmidt provides a very detailed comparison of the stages of development of several stories, from the handwritten notes of Jacob and Wilhelm and their amanuenses through the different editions of the published collection.   Some changes are microscopic (*Hochmut* becomes *Stolz*, akin to changing "pride" to "haughtiness"), some are radical. [31] Rölleke's study[32] of the Grimms' at work is broader, but equally meticulous.   In his preface Rölleke states that the stories in this

---

[31] Schmidt, *passim.*
[32] Rölleke 1977, passim.

collection are transcribed from the Grimms' handwritten notes. Examination of the tales reveals that they are edited at least to the extent of filling out abbreviations, e.g.

v<on> d seltenen Wein geben

("give o[f] th[e] strange wine")

Many of the forty-eight tales (some are fragments) are new, but a few are variant versions of the "canonical," that is, seventh edition *KHM*. *Der Zaunkönig* is given in dialect, and the comparison with the final version is an instructive look over the Grimms' shoulder.

Rölleke's extensive list of Grimm publications gives him enormous credibility, but the reader will recall that he is firmly in the mainstream of the way we look at the Brothers Grimm: thus, there is little to fear from the lunatic fringe, but on the other hand alertness is called for, lest fruitful anomalies get swept under the rug. We see what we are prepared to see, after all. To Rölleke, then, the *KHM* are authentically rooted in folk tradition, although they exist only in edited, that is, in altered, form. (Perhaps I should say to Rölleke in 1977; as we shall see, his 1993 study is somewhat more skeptical.) Rölleke's definition of folk tradition is obviously broad, including both the original forms of the stories, as told by informants of average to very little education, and their written versions, as recorded by the very intellectual Grimms. A strength of this collection, as always in Rölleke's work, is his thoroughness and clarity. A native speaker of German might find his explanatory notes just right; but for a native English speaker, even one who knows enough German to know that Rapunzel is a kind of lettuce, puzzled by this or that dialect term, though, a little more help would have been nice. The main help this collection offers is as a guide to how the Brothers Grimm operated with reference to their editorial policy on dialect; using it fully will involve thinking backward, from standard German into the Black Forest of regionalisms, but at least it provides a model. It is a good reference for detailed examination of the stories in question, but only up to a point. The reader still has no way of knowing whether the stories went bourgeois on the lips of the informant or the pen of the transcriber.

This brings us back to Fink. It may be true that toiling masses tell one kind of story, and their Oppressors another. Fink takes it as self-evident; I do not, except as a plausible, or, if you will, an arguable generalization. In the case of the Krause stories, we have noted that soldier's tales are told with a soldier's vocabulary, and that the details of this soldierly "accent" are instructive.

Instead of building a mosaic of these details, however, Fink argues *a priori*: the stories are amoral (that is, they are judged on whether or not they benefit the hero), so they must relate to the lower class. Indeed? In Fink's view, the world of the *Fairy Tales* is a crude, nuanceless struggle between haves and have-nots, or even between have-nots and have-littles, and in which the *Tales* themselves are only homespun agitprop. To each his own; yet Fink's thrashing around in his theoretical Black Forest seems to have led him full circle to the simplistic approach I have described at the beginning of this chapter: that *KHM* seem to belong to a dream world, out of space and time, as orderly as a string of pearls, "as is, where, is."

(A final note of protest before we leave Fink, concerning his airy, New Age, patently silly characterization of Christianity as "phallocratic."[33]   The preferred term, for over thirty years before Fink wrote, had been "patriarchal," which was inaccurate enough; "phallocratic," however, is incorrect to the point of inviting waggery: if Christianity were indeed "phallocratic" it would stand to reason that there would be a flood of would-be phallocrator converts for a while, but upon learning that Christianity is a Biedermeier religion after all, the enthusiasm would wane.)

A close literary, as opposed to theoretical, examination of Krause's tales leads us to another parameter that is much more important than these retouches, however, a parameter potentially fatal to the Grimms' integrity, that of literary antecedents.

In §20, *Das tapfere Schneiderlein* ("the brave little tailor") the hero is required to catch a unicorn, which he does when the unicorn's horn gets stuck in a tree, leaving the creature helpless, at the tailor's mercy.   Similar episodes occur in two other sources known to the Grimms: a literary antecedent by one Martin Montanus[34] that first appeared between 1557 and 1566, called *Von einem könig, schneyder, rysen und wilden schwein* ("about a king, tailor, giants and wild boar"); the second was ex-sergeant Krause's, *Herr Fix-und-Fertig*.   This unlikely convergence of the twain presents a puzzle: Krause, after all, was no antiquarian, and Montanus wrote more than two centuries before that veteran was born.   Does this double occurrence of the unicorn story (in a spoken version and a literary one) vindicate the Grimms' assumption that the oral tradition of their day preserves the traditions of an earlier day?

---

[33] Fink 156.
[34] Rölleke 1977, 38.

This question must be prefaced by another, that of the honesty of the Brothers Grimm: *falsus in uno, falsus in omnibus* (false in one particular, false across the board), after all, so if their veracity is in doubt, it may be that Krause never told them the story, that their account was just genteel, Romantic flim-flam. This may be called the "Ellis question," since John M. Ellis asked it most insistently in *One Fairy Story too Many*.

> ...during the course of this study it will become evident that the changes introduced by the Grimms were far fore than mere stylistic matters, and that the facts of their editorial procedure, taken together with the evidence as to their sources, are sufficient completely to undermine any notion that the Grimms' fairy tales are of folk, or peasant, or even German origin.[35]

Editor Rölleke, in his early days a great admirer of the Brothers, would later follow up on this line of attack by a detailed compilation: parallel passages of Grimm and earlier works, both contemporary, medieval and classical, show similarities so strong, down to words and turns of phrase, that suggest that the Grimms manufactured some of their tales by simply stealing and modernizing older texts, some even as well-known as Hans Sachs.[36]

Well and good; yet, as I write this, I glance across the room at my music stand, and see Bartók's *44 Duets for two violins*

---

[35] Ellis 12.
[36] Rölleke 1998, *passim.*

(Boosey & Hawkes 1960); Béla Bartók, or rather Bartók and his collaborator Zoltán Kodály, as ethnomusicologists are entirely analogous to the Brothers Grimm as folklorists. On one hand, they were pure collectors, even more so than the Grimms, tramping out in the woods in search of Eastern European peasant songs; on the other, they were disseminators of what they collected, both in scholarly media and in popular ones, like Bartók's *44 Duets,* which have all sorts of un-peasant counterpoint and harmony, and un-peasant globe-trotting (#5 is a Slovak song, #6 is Hungarian, #7 is Walachian). Does this mean that the folksongs do not exist? Certainly not: it means that each relayer of the folksong leaves his mark, and that mark can be either very naive or very arty. Would these folksong arrangements survive Ellis's challenge? For that matter, do the *KHM* survive it? For balance, a passage from Maria Tatar's *The Hard Facts of the Grimms' Fairy Tales.*

> Every storyteller has a unique repertory of tales, one developed in collaboration with an audience... The successful retelling of a tale requires the narrator to take the measure of his listeners... Thus the teller of tales works in concert with his audience to create popular tales.[37]

This suggests a thought experiment that can be applied to *KHM*: let us say that there is a story where a pregnant girl poisons the aristocrat who has abandoned her. If the cook in the household of the Hassenpflug family (the source of many *Tales*) is relaying

---

[37] Tatar 25.

this story to young Johanna Isabella ("Jeanette") Hassenpflug (1791-1860), the poisoning (a subject cooks would avoid) may be altered to a hex; when Jeanette passes the story on to the Grimms, she may bowdlerize it to avoid its attendant "Men are Rats" digression.   What is so unnatural, then, about the Brothers Grimm's emendations for a reading audience?   It is still the same tale.   One may argue that less is more, or invoke the saying about "too many cooks," but those are not questions of validity, but of editing, where there is plenty of room for individual tastes.

With this in mind, let us return to our unicorns.   Krause's account of the capture first:[38] the confident Fix-und-Fertig (he begins his first labor *Linksum!*   [forward march!]) is advised by the ravens (for whom he on a previous occasion had a horse killed, so they wouldn't go hungry):

> *'Noch eine Weile geduld!   Jetzt liegt das Einhorn und schläft, aber nicht auf der scheelen Seite.   Wenn es sich herumdreht, dann wollen wir ihm das eine gute Auge, das es hat, auspicken.   Dann ist es blind und wird in seiner Wut gegen die Bäume rennen und mit seinem Horn sich festspießen.'*
> ("Patient a little longer!   Now the unicorn is lying down and sleeping, but not on the squint side.   When it drags itself around, then we'll pick out the one good eye that it has.   Then it is blind and in its frenzy will run against the trees and lance itself fast with its horn.")

---

[38]   Bolte & Polívka 2:21

Two details in this cold-blooded episode mark the teller as an unlettered military man: his grammar (*Dann ist es blind* ["then it is blind"] instead of *Dann würde es blind sein* ["then it would be blind"], and his terminology: *Spieß* is the Napoleonic era word for "lance" or "pike;" it is incidentally the slang term for "sergeant major," Krause's former rank. One notes without enthusiasm that being blinded by birds also occurs in §58, *Der Hund und der Sperling* ("the dog and the sparrow") and in §21, *Aschenputtel* ("Cinderella").

Montanus's version[39] is in a quaint sort of older German, but still intelligible.

> *Der schneider war sein wol zu friden, nam ein strickelein, gieng zum wald, befalhe seinen zugeordneten heraussen zuwarten, er wolt allein hinein. Spatzieret also im walde umbher, in dem ersicht er das einhorn gegen ime daher springen der meinung in umzubringen. Der schneider aber war nit unbehendt, wartet, biß das einhorn gar nahe zu im kam; und als es nahe bey im was, stelt er sich hinder den baum, dabei er zu aller nächst war. Das einhorn aber, so sich in vollem lauff nicht wenden kundt, mit dem horn in baum lieff und also darinn unverwendt stecken blyb.*

("The tailor was calm, took a length of rope, went to the forest, obeyed his orders to wait out there, he wished to go alone. Thus he rambled in the woods, in which he saw the unicorn charge with the intention of killing him. The tailor, though, was not caught off-guard, waited until the unicorn came quite near to him; and as it was upon him, he

---

[39] Rölleke 50.

placed himself behind the tree he was nearest.   The unicorn, however, being at top speed, could not turn, ran into the tree with its horn and remained stuck.")

It will be noted that the final version of the unicorn hunt in *Das tapfere Schneiderlein* resembles Montanus more than Krause.   The "Ellis question" pops up again, but in this case the matter is resolved broadly pro-Grimm: true, they may have used the un-peasant Montanus as a secondary source, but they could have done so knowing that the story did survive among the common people, as witness the fact that Krause knew a gruesome version of it, and were thus justified in publishing an arty version of it.   The same is true of the "seven at one blow" motif, whose source is identified as "the Hassenpflugs."[40]   Yet the "...at one blow" idea is widely attested contemporary with the Montanus material:[41]   from 1575 there is *Ich will euch tödten wie die Mucken, neun in eim Streich, wie jener Schneider* ("I'll kill you like gnats, nine at one blow, like that tailor"); in 1577 *Hörst nicht vom tapfern Schneiderknecht, Der drei in aim Streich tödtet schlecht* ("Haven't you heard of the brave tailor-servant, who killed three at one blow, flat"); and a poem from 1593 speaks of *Syben in eim Streich auff eim Hauffen* ("syven in one blow inn one heapp").   There is even a 1527 quotation from Luther, although it is less apropos: *sie schlahen damit allemal tausent auff einen Schlag tod* ("with it they would strike a thousand dead at one stroke").   The Grimms credited the Hassenpflugs with the motif, however; it is plausible that

---

[40] Bolte & Polívka 1:148.
[41] Bolte & Polívka 1:149

their story did use that turn of phrase, and that its existence in centuries past was regarded by the Grimms as an argument for the existence and authenticity of a cultural continuum.

There are times, however, when " the Ellis question" hits the mark. "The Hassenpflugs" may be a slightly nebulous term, since it involves a number of individuals; let us focus on one, Johanna, or Jeanette. She is credited with several tales, but it takes only a cursory glance to see that her stories have been badly skewed: the tale reveals the teller, and examination of the tales attributed to her reveals impossibly contradictory traits. She is credited with §36 *Tischchen deck dich, Goldesel und Knüppel aus dem Sack* ("table be set, gold-donkey and stick from the sack"), with §41 *Herr Korbes* ("Mr. Korbes"), and with §67 *Die zwölf Jäger* ("the twelve hunters"). Let us set aside my attribution of §36 to Krause for a moment; taking the traditional attribution at face value for the moment will be instructive. The first and third of these are finished tales, in the artistic sense, but §41 *Herr Korbes* is worth examination precisely because it is so artless, even to the point of being idiotic. A collection of animals and notions (needles, a millstone) go to visit Herr Korbes, and array themselves as booby-traps throughout his house, causing him injury and humiliation. There is no reason given for the pranks; in the second edition a lame concluding sentence was tacked on, that *der Herr Korbes muß ein recht böser Mann gewesen sein* ("Mr. Korbes must have been a really bad man"), which implies that it had occurred to the Grimms that this incoherent mayhem called for some justification.

The tale reveals the teller. Jeanette is credited with this puerile story, but also with the very arty *zwölf Jäger* and the almost plagiaristic *Tischchen*, which is obviously a knockoff of Krause's *Der Ranzen, das Hütlein und das Hörnlein* ("the knapsack, the hat and the bugle"). If the tale does reveal the teller, then the reader must conclude either that Jeanette had multiple personalities or that something fishy is going on. The English translator evidently had his suspicions, since the Grimms wrote to him on the subject of *Herr Korbes* in 1823. Their reply displays just the sort of disingenuousness that Ellis complains of: they allege that the very name *Korbes* would fill German children with fear, and thus there was no need to establish the man's *mala fides*.[42] This sounded like malarkey to me, since the only German word I know of that it resembles is *Korb* ("basket") and equally unthreatening compounds containing it (the ribcage is a *Brustkorb*, for example); I am not a German, though, not even in the remotest corners of my family tree, and so was prepared to leave the door open to the possibility that the Grimms were right; no longer, however, since, by one of those happy accidents of Fate, back in December of 2000 I happened to meet a real, live German – named Körbling! I put the question to him as to just what sort of terror the name Korbes would inspire in German children. This cultured Heidelberger confirmed my suspicions: there is nothing frightening about the name at all, and that has been the answer I have received every time I have asked it since. Much as I admire Grimm/Jekyll, here I must concur with Ellis as to the existence of Grimm/Hyde. And yet... and yet...

Must a classic be simon-pure? True, there are instances where the Grimms fibbed, fudged and flirted with mild literary

---

[42] Bolte & Polívka 1:375

skullduggery; but little was lost, since the cultural background material that they excised can be retrieved from other sources, and much was gained, since the "permanent laryngitis to the unheard" is in fact relieved by what they preserved; and the form of what they preserved gave Dorothea Viehmann and Johann Friedrich Krause a greater audience than either could ever have dreamed of.

Bibliography

Anonymous. *The Vita Merlini.* Parry, J. J., ed. and trans. Urbana, Ill.: The University of Illinois, 1925.

Baildon, H. Bellyse, ed. *The Works of Shakespeare: The Lamentable Tragedy of Titus Andronicus.* Methuen, 1904.

Bate, Jonathan ed. *Titus Andronicus.* Routledge, 1995

Berschin, Walter, ed. *Hrotsvit: Opera Omnia.* Munich and Leipzig, K. G. Saur, 2001.

Bertram, Paul. *Shakespeare and the Two Noble Kinsmen.* Rutgers, 1965.

Binyon, Laurence. *The Madness of Merlin.* London: Macmillan 1947.

Blackburn, Francis A., ed. *Exodus and Daniel: Two Old English Poems Preserved in Ms. Junius 11 in the Bodleian Library of the University of Oxford, England.* D.C. Heath and Co., 1907.

Blake, N.F., ed. *Phoenix.* Manchester University Press, 1964.

Boas, Frederick S. *Shakespere and his Predecessors.* Gordian Press, 1968 [1896].

Bolte, Johannes and Polívka, Georg. *Anmerkungen zu den Kinder- u. Hausmärchen der Brüder Grimm.* Hildesheim: Georg Olms Verlagsbuchhandlungen, 1983.

Bradley, S.A.J., trans. and ed. *Anglo-Saxon Poetry.* Everyman, 1998.

Brook, Peter. *The Shifting Point 1946-1987.* Harper & Row, 1987.

Brown, Phyllis, Linda A. McMillin and Katharina M. Wilson, eds. *Hrotsvit of Gandersheim: Contexts, Identities, Affinities, and Performances.* University of Toronto Press 2004

Butler, Sister Mary Marguerite, R.S.M. *Hrotsvitha: The Theatricality of Her Plays.* New York, Philosophical Library 1960

Casariego, J.E., *El Periplo de Hannón de Cartago*, Marsiega, 1947

Chambers, E. K., "The First Illustration to 'Shakespeare.'" The Library, 4th ser., 5 (1925):   326-30.

_____. *William Shakespeare: A Study of Facts and Problems.* (two vols.) Oxford, 1988.

Clarke, Basil. *Life of Merlin.* Cardiff: University of Wales Press, 1973.

Clubb, Merrel Dare, ed. *Christ and Satan: An Old English Poem.* New Haven: Yale University Press, 1925.

Cohn, Alfred. *Shakespeare in Germany in the Sixteenth and Seventeenth Centuries: An Account of English Actors in Germany and the Netherlands and of the Plays Performed by Them During the Same Period.* Haskell House Publishers, Ltd. New York, 1971.

Crawford, Charles. "The Date and Authenticity of Titus Andronicus." Jahrbuch der Deutschen Shakespeare-Gesellschaft. XIII [1900]. Vaduz, Kraus Reprint 1963.

Dickins, Bruce, and Ross, Alan S.C., eds. *The Dream of the Rood.* Appleton-Century-Crofts, 1966.

Dronke, Peter. *Women Writers of the Middle Ages: A Critical Study of Texts from Perpetua (✝ 203) to Marguerite Porete (✝ 1310).* Cambridge University Press, 1984.

Ellis, John M.   *One Fairy Story too Many.*   University of Chicago Press, 1983.

Fink, Gonthier-Louis. "The Fairy Tales of the Grimm's Sergeant of Dragoons J. F. Krause as Reflecting the Needs and Wishes of the Common People," in McGlathery, below.

Fletcher, Richard.   *Moorish Spain.*   New York.   Henry Holt, 1992.

Frazer, Winifred.   "Henslowe's 'NE'   Notes and Queries 236 (1991):   34-5.

Gollancz, Israel, ed.   *Shakespeare's Tragedy of Titus Andronicus.* Cambridge University Press, 1994.

Gradon, P.O.E., ed.   *Cynewulf's 'Elene.'*   University of Exeter, 1977.

Greene, Robert.   *The Tragical Reign of Selimus.*   Alexander B. Grosart, ed.   London, J.M. Dent, 1898.

Grimm, Brüder. *Kinder- und Hausmärchen.   Ausgabe letzter Hand Mit einem Anhang sämmtlicher nicht in allen Auflagen veröffentlicher Märchen.* Rölleke, Heinz, ed. Philipp Reclam, jun., 1980.

Grimm, Brüder. *Kinder- und Hausmärchen, Nach der Großen Ausgabe von 1857, textkritisch revidert, kommentiert und durch Register erschlossen.* Uther, Hans-Jörg, ed. Eugen Diederichs Verlag, 1996.

Grimm, Jacob. *Selbstbiographie: Ausgewählte Schriften, Reden und Abhandlungen.* Wyss, Ulrich, ed. Deutscher Taschenbuch Verlag 1984

Gurr, Andrew. *The Shakespearean Stage 1574-1642.* Cambridge, 1970.

Halliday, F. E. *A Shakespeare Companion.* Duckworth, 1964.

Henry of Huntingdon. *Historia Anglorum, The History of the English People, 1000-1154 / Henry of Huntingdon; translated from the Latin, with an introduction and notes by Diana Greenway.* Oxford University Press, 2002.

Hill, Boyd. H., Jr. *Medieval Monarchy in Action: The German Empire for Henry I to Henry IV.* Barnes and Noble, 1972.

Hrotsvit von Gandersheim. *Sämtliche Dichtungen.* Winkler, 1966

Hughes, Alan ed. *Titus Andronicus.* Cambridge University Press, 1994.

Ingrao, Charles W. *The Hessian mercenary state: Ideas, institutions and reform under Frederick II, 1760-1785.* Cambridge University Press, 1987.

Isidore of Seville, Saint. *Etymologiae.* ed. W.M. Lindsay. Oxford University Press, 1966.

Jansohn, Christa, ed. *German Shakespeare Studies at the Turn of the Twenty-First Century.* Newark: University of Delaware Press, 2006.

McGlathery, James M., *Grimms' Fairy Tales: A History of Criticism on a Popular Classic.* Camden House, 1993.

Massai, Sonia, ed. *Titus Andronicus.* Penguin, 2001.

Maxwell, J.C. *Titus Andronicus.* Methuen, 1968.

Metz, G. Harold. *Shakespeare's Earliest Tragedy: Studies in Titus Andronicus.* Farleigh Dickinson University Press, 1996.

Murray, Barbara A. *Restoration Shakespeare: Viewing the Voice.* Farleigh Dickinson University Press, 2001.

_____. *Shakespeare Adaptations from the Restoration: Five Plays.* Farleigh Dickinson University Press, 2005.

O'Callaghan, Joseph F. *A History of Medieval Spain.* Cornell University Press, 1975

Peele, George. The Works of George Peele. A. H. Bullen, ed. 2 vols. Kennikat Press, 1966.

Potter, Simeon. *Our Language.* Penguin, 1951.

Raidonis Bates, Laura. "Hamlet under Imperialist Rule." Lituanus 43:3, Fall 1997. www.lituanus.org /1997/97_3_04.htm

Ravenscroft, Edward. *Titus Andronicus.* Cornmarket Press, 1969.

Ridley M. R., ed. *Titus Andronicus.* E. P. Dutton, 1934.

Robertson, J. M. *An Introduction to the Study of the Shakespeare Canon: Proceeding on the Problem of "Titus Andronicus."* Greenwood Press1970 [1924].

Rölleke, Heinz. *Die Märchen der Brüder Grimm; Eine Einführung.* Artemis Verlag, 1985.

_____. *Grimms Märchen, Ausgewählt und mit einem Kommantar versehen.* Suhrkamp, 1998.

_____. *Grimms Märchen und ihre Quellen: Die literarischen Vorlagen der Grimmschen Märchen synoptisch vorgestellt und kommentiert.* Wissenschaftlische Verlag Trier, 1998

_____. *Märchen aus dem Nachlaß der Brüder Grimm.* Bouvier, 1977.

Schlueter, June. "Rereading the Peacham Drawing." Shakespeare Quarterly 50 (1999): 171-84.

Schmidt, Kurt   *Die Entwicklung der Grimmschen Kinder- und Hausmärchen nebst einem kritischen Text*.   Max Niemeyer Verlag Tübingen 1973.

Skupin, Michael.   "Merlin in the Works of E.A. Robinson and Laurence Binyon."   Unpublished dissertation.   University of Houston, 2003.

Skupin, Jon.   Personal communication.

Smith, Colin.   *Christians and Moors in Spain: Vol. 1:   711-1100*.   Aris & Phillips, 1988.

Smith, F. Kinchin, and Melluish, T.W., eds.   *Catullus: Selections from the Poems*.   George Allen & Unwin, 1966.

St. John, Christopher, tr.   *The Plays of Roswitha*.   New York, Benjamin Blom, 1966.

Tatar, Maria. *The Hard Facts of the Grimms' Fairy Tales*. Princeton: Princeton University Press, 1987.

Taylor, Peter K.   *Indentured to Liberty: Peasant Life and the Hessian Military State, 1688-1815*.   Cornell University Press, 1994.

Tolan, John V.   *Saracens: Islam in the Medieval European Imagination*.   New York, Columbia University Press, 2002.

Van Lennep, William, ed.   *The London Stage 1660-1800, Part I: 1660-1700*.   Southern Illinois University Press, Carbondale, Illinois 1965.

Vickers, Brian.   *Shakespeare, Co-Author: A Historical Study of Five Collaborative Plays*.   Oxford University Press, 2002.

Wailes, Stephen L.   *Spirituality and Politics in the Works of Hrotsvit of Gandersheim*.   Susquehanna University Press, 2006

Waith, Eugene M. ed. *Titus Andronicus.* Oxford University Press, 1984

Wilson, John Dover, ed. *Titus Andronicus.* Cambridge University Press, 1948.

Witherspoon, A. M., ed. *The Tragedy of Titus Andronicus.* Yale University Press, 1926.

Wright, Neil, ed. *The Historia regum Britannie of Geoffrey of Monmouth.* Cambridge University Press, 1985.

Zedler, Johann Heinrich. *Grosses vollständiges Universal-Lexicon.* Akademische Druck- und Verlagsanstalt, 1961-64.

語言文學類　AG0110

Anonymity in Western Literature

作　　者 / Michael Skupin
發 行 人 / 宋政坤
執行編輯 / 詹靚秋
圖文排版 / 鄭維心
封面設計 / 陳佩蓉
數位轉譯 / 徐真玉　沈裕閔
圖書銷售 / 林怡君
法律顧問 / 毛國樑　律師
出版印製 / 秀威資訊科技股份有限公司
　　　　　臺北市內湖區瑞光路 583 巷 25 號 1 樓
　　　　　電話：02-2657-9211　　　　傳真：02-2657-9106
　　　　　E-mail：service@showwe.com.tw
經 銷 商 / 紅螞蟻圖書有限公司
　　　　　臺北市內湖區舊宗路二段 121 巷 28、32 號 4 樓
　　　　　電話：02-2795-3656　　　　傳真：02-2795-4100
　　　　　http://www.e-redant.com

2009 年 4 月 BOD 一版
定價：250 元

讀　者　回　函　卡

感謝您購買本書，為提升服務品質，煩請填寫以下問卷，收到您的寶貴意見後，我們會仔細收藏記錄並回贈紀念品，謝謝！

1.您購買的書名：＿＿＿＿＿＿＿＿＿＿＿＿＿＿＿＿＿＿＿

2.您從何得知本書的消息？

　　□網路書店　　□部落格　　□資料庫搜尋　　□書訊　□電子報　□書店

　　□平面媒體　　□ 朋友推薦　　□網站推薦　□其他＿＿＿＿＿＿

3.您對本書的評價：(請填代號　1.非常滿意 2.滿意 3.尚可 4.再改進)

　　封面設計＿＿　　版面編排＿＿　　內容＿＿　　文/譯筆＿＿　　價格＿＿

4.讀完書後您覺得：

　　□很有收獲　　□有收獲　　□收獲不多　　□沒收獲

5.您會推薦本書給朋友嗎？

　　□會　　□不會，為什麼？＿＿＿＿＿＿＿＿＿＿＿＿＿＿＿＿＿

6.其他寶貴的意見：＿＿＿＿＿＿＿＿＿＿＿＿＿＿＿＿＿＿＿＿

　　＿＿＿＿＿＿＿＿＿＿＿＿＿＿＿＿＿＿＿＿＿＿＿＿＿＿＿＿

　　＿＿＿＿＿＿＿＿＿＿＿＿＿＿＿＿＿＿＿＿＿＿＿＿＿＿＿＿

　　＿＿＿＿＿＿＿＿＿＿＿＿＿＿＿＿＿＿＿＿＿＿＿＿＿＿＿＿

讀者基本資料

姓名：＿＿＿＿＿＿＿＿＿＿　　年齡：＿＿＿＿　　性別：□女　□男

聯絡電話：＿＿＿＿＿＿＿＿＿　E-mail：＿＿＿＿＿＿＿＿＿＿

地址：＿＿＿＿＿＿＿＿＿＿＿＿＿＿＿＿＿＿＿＿＿＿＿＿＿＿

學歷：□高中(含)以下　　□高中　　□專科學校　　□大學

　　　□研究所(含)以上 □其他＿＿＿＿＿＿＿

職業：□製造業 □金融業 □資訊業 □軍警 □傳播業 □自由業

　　　□服務業 □公務員 □教職　　□學生 □其他＿＿＿＿＿＿

To：114

台北市內湖區瑞光路 583 巷 25 號 1 樓

秀威資訊科技股份有限公司　　　收

寄件人姓名：

寄件人地址：□□□

(請沿線對摺寄回,謝謝!)

秀威與 BOD

BOD（Books On Demand）是數位出版的大趨勢，秀威資訊率先運用 POD 數位印刷設備來生產書籍，並提供作者全程數位出版服務，致使書籍產銷零庫存，知識傳承不絕版，目前已開闢以下書系：

一、BOD 學術著作—專業論述的閱讀延伸
二、BOD 個人著作—分享生命的心路歷程
三、BOD 旅遊著作—個人深度旅遊文學創作
四、BOD 大陸學者—大陸專業學者學術出版
五、POD 獨家經銷—數位產製的代發行書籍

BOD 秀威網路書店：www.showwe.com.tw
政府出版品網路書店：www.govbooks.com.tw

　　永不絕版的故事・自己寫・永不休止的音符・自己唱